MW00441000

The Price of Creation

From the Historian Tales

By Lance Conrad

To the students of Springville High,

Lance Conrad

10-8-14

The following is a work of fiction. All characters and events portrayed herein are the invention of a brilliant creative mind, any similarity to any real persons or occurrences is purely coincidental. More or less.

The Price of Creation

Cover art by Noel Sellon

ISBN: 978-0-9910230-0-4

Printed in the United States of America

For Misty, who reminds me that the destination doesn't matter if the journey isn't fun.

Chapter 1

I am the Historian, I am immortal, I am ageless, I am nameless. I am carried by my own feet through times and worlds to witness great stories

This is one such story.

I remember that it was a beautiful day. The magic of a blue sky and singing birds has still not lost its allure, even after all these years. It was the kind of day when walking is a pleasure, especially if you have nowhere in particular to go. The landscape spread out in front of me for endless miles, the long grass and wildflowers waving softly in a warm summer breeze. The ground felt soft under my bare feet, not even so much as a rock disturbed the hypnotic rhythm of my steps.

The land I was walking in showed no signs of civilization. There were no farms or buildings to be seen anywhere. Given the lack of such markers of civilization, I was surprised when a wall appeared in the distance, unlike any I had seen before. The wall stretched as far as I could see in both directions. What this wall was designed to keep in or keep out, I couldn't begin to guess, but even as I approached from afar, an old curiosity was starting to itch its way into my mind.

When I arrived at the wall, I was astounded by the magnitude of it.

Whether for keeping out or keeping in, the wall was well designed for its purpose. The stone it was made out of was solid and the blocks were fit together so that no mortar was used, the rocks simply fit together. If it weren't for the different types of rock used in the wall, I might have assumed that they had somehow just used one rock and that it was cracked. The sides were entirely smooth. A person couldn't have fit the point of a knife into the seams of the stones, much less fingers for climbing. The wall was easily three times as high as my head. The top was lined with an ingenious network of sharpened stones and poles.

The poles were arranged like wheels, all of the spokes sharpened. They were set onto a long rod that ran the length of the wall, like so many spiked wheels on a single axle. Any person trying to get over the wall would be impaled and then the wheels would rotate under his weight, throwing him back on whatever side he had come from.

The stones at the top of the wall were equally treacherous. Small, sharp stones bristled over the top, worked into the stone of the wall itself. It was hard to tell from where I stood, but the stones looked like jaggedly sharpened obsidian, sharp enough to cut through flesh or ropes or anything else that came in contact with them. With those stones covering the top of the wall like a porcupine, no one would even get close enough to try their luck with the poles.

Each defense complemented another, insuring that nothing would come over the wall. I walked along for hours, but never saw any gates. Whoever had built this wall had absolutely no intention of ever crossing to the other side. Maybe there was some secret method of passage. If there was one lesson to be learned from the ages, it was to never underestimate human cunning.

I had walked along the wall for most of the day before I saw any sign of civilization. The sun was already dipping onto the far mountains when my eyes finally caught a glimpse of a small settlement. They would have to know something. A wall like that would be visible for some distance.

As I neared the village, I noticed the same level of craftsmanship in their dwellings as that which built the wall. These people knew how to work with their hands, that was obvious.

When I entered the village, the women scattered, screaming as they ran from me. Others shouted warnings and urgent commands to their children, who needed no prompting in their flight.

It was human nature to be suspicious of strangers, and I had seldom entered any new place when I was not viewed with guarded glances. Still, this reaction was an extreme case. This was closer to a mindless panic. Most alarming was what they were yelling as they fled.

"Destroyer!"

I stopped where I stood and held my hands out in what I hoped was a friendly gesture. I was beginning to think I had made a mistake. My suspicions were confirmed when the men of the village appeared, holding various farm implements menacingly in their hands. I raised my hands higher to show that I was unarmed and peaceful. Most of the men only gripped their makeshift weapons tighter. Their fear was tangible in the air.

One man separated himself from the crowd. This man was truly one to be reckoned with. The first image that came to my head as I saw him was one of a mountain, massive, invulnerable, and completely calm. This one was not afraid like the others. One of the men behind him, a man with small eyes and a deep scowl hissed a warning at the other man that I could not hear. The large man ignored him and continued to walk toward me, showing his own empty hands as a sign of peace.

I smiled inwardly, that man needed a weapon like a bear needed a knife. I had little doubt in my mind that he could have crushed me with one hand. His actions seemed to be sincere, however, and I tried to look as peaceful and harmless as I could in return.

When he was within hearing distance, he spoke, his voice rolling like a low thunder,

"Who are you and what are your intentions here?"

"He's a Destroyer! Get back here, Aric! We can deal with him." The small-eyed man was looking even angrier. His tone was imperious and commanding, but it slid like rain off the mountain of a man that stood before me.

There was something different about the small-eyed man as well. He didn't seem very afraid either; he appeared more confused than anything, covering his bewilderment with his angry ranting. I looked back to the large man and answered his question.

"I am simply a traveler, I just wanted a drink of water, maybe to take a moment and wash the dust of the road from my feet." I replied.

"He's lying! Grab him, Aric!" The man's tone was getting frantic, but it could not touch the calm of Aric. He turned his large head to answer the man.

"You should not be so hasty, Saddhan, he carries no weapons, he's not dressed like a Destroyer, he doesn't even have a

4

Stone."

I took the opportunity while they were arguing to get a better look at the men facing me. They were of average height; I guessed that only Aric would be above six feet if they were to be measured. Most of them had blond or light brown hair that blended well with their tanned faces. They had obviously just run in from the fields to defend their homes against me, many were still panting hard from the sudden exertion. Dirt caked around their arms and feet and their faces wore the grime of a long day in the fields. Their clothes were the honest, rugged type you'd expect on farmers, though of the highest quality.

Above all, though, these were frightened men. Even though it was a crowd of men against one unarmed traveler, they didn't even seem confident that they would win should it come to fighting.

I wondered what he meant about the Stone I apparently didn't have. It was then that I noticed that every man surrounding me wore a gem of sorts around his neck like an amulet. They were like clear crystals and came in a variety of colors, although their shapes were all identical, a perfect oval, almost like a robin's egg. Aric's Stone was a deep blue, not unlike deep water. I noted Saddhan's red Stone as he started ranting again.

"It is just more of their treachery, Aric! We should kill this one before others come, quickly, before he can say anything else." Saddhan seemed especially insistent that I should not be allowed to speak.

"Is human life truly so cheap to you, Saddhan?" A look of fatigue crossed Aric's eyes, as if this were a battle that had been fought many times. "A traveler is requesting hospitality, and I intend to offer it. If he proves hostile in any way, I will take full responsibility.

"Besides," Aric added as an afterthought. "If he is a Destroyer, he is alone and he might be able to tell us how they are getting over the wall."

Saddhan looked angrier than ever, but he could feel his support starting to drain away as most of the men around him started to lower their weapons. They looked all too happy to transfer this newcomer over to Aric. Great craftsmen these men might be, but there wasn't a single warrior among them.

Saddhan fumed for a moment, studying my face and clothing intently; then his demeanor changed abruptly and he lowered his weapon to the ground, lifting his other hand in welcome.

"Of course! We should never let our hospitality be questioned, if this good man needs help on his road, our community will be glad to provide it and see him safely on his way."

I nodded my thanks. I had seen his kind hundreds of times; he was a politician. Whatever the crowd wanted would be his newest brilliant idea.

Aric shifted his gaze from Saddhan back to me, extending his hand,

"Welcome to Surac, stranger. I'm sorry for the misunderstanding, but I'm sure you understand why we have to be careful."

"Well, I'm from a land very far away." I responded as I took his hand. I was struck by the power of the man. I was sure that his hand only stopped in its grip because he chose to stop it there, not from any opposing pressure from my hand or the bones in it. "I don't actually know of your troubles here, but I would be happy to hear more about them."

"Really?" The big man's eyes suddenly lit up like a child's. The man who had stood like a bear against his fellow villagers now eagerly pressed for any kind of information with a wide-eyed innocence that was very disarming. "I have walked long distances, but I have never even seen any sign of anything beyond our own villages. What can you tell me about your land? Do you have a different language? How is it that you speak ours? Say something in your own language, please."

I smiled, this man would have made a good historian, his curiosity was almost overwhelming.

"Well, if you have traveled far in your exploring, I'm sure you appreciate how badly I need to rest at the moment." I hinted.

Aric's eyes dropped and his hands snuck behind his back.

"I'm sorry, I'm forgetting myself, you must be hungry and exhausted," Aric suddenly looked confused, looking at my empty shoulders, then down to my feet. "Don't you have a pack or something? You aren't even wearing shoes."

I laughed lightly, "You are indeed observant, that is one of the reasons I decided to come in. Someone has robbed me. I was hoping to maybe stay here a short while and work for some new provisions, I'm afraid I have no money."

"Not another word!" Aric bellowed. "I understand completely. You follow me, and don't worry about paying, I'll give you all the provisions you need just to hear some of your stories from your land." Aric had turned and started to lumber away before he even finished speaking. I found myself almost jogging to keep up with his quick, long strides.

"Ok," I replied with a well-worn lie, "but I'm really not much of a story-teller."

Aric looked a little sad at the comment, but his enthusiasm was relentless. "Don't worry about that. I just want to hear what is beyond where the sun sets. Lauria always laughs at me, but I still get restless here, I want to see the far side of a mountain, even knowing that it will look just like the one we see. Sorry, I'm talking crazy, what will you think?"

I smiled again. "Don't worry, I understand all too well, why else would I be in your lands?"

Aric smiled gratefully, happy to have found someone who shared in his interest.

"Most people in our villages aren't curious at all, they are happy to live out their lives in whatever life their Stone leads them to. Oh, here we are."

We had walked outside the cluster of houses that made up the village. Aric's house stood alone, a ways off from the village. It was as well-crafted as the others. One difference was the presence of a couple of smaller buildings next to his house, workshops of some kind, I guessed.

"I'm a blacksmith," He started to explain. "Although they are very grateful for my services, nobody is very happy to have a blacksmith as a neighbor, too much smoke and noise."

Aric pushed his way into the modestly sized house, made out of the same stone as the wall. A very pretty, and very pregnant, woman rose up out of her chair as quickly as a woman in her condition can. She crossed the floor quickly to embrace her husband. I was impressed by the gentleness that Aric displayed as he placed his massive hands softly on her small back, returning her embrace. They made an interesting couple. His size and bulk contrasted sharply against her slim form. She still looked very strong, however, and her feminine hands still bore traces of calluses. Aric straightened and motioned to me.

"This is my wife, Lauria. Lauria, this is…" Suddenly Aric looked very lost. "Odd, I don't remember your name, friend."

"Don't worry, your memory still serves you well, I never told it to you. It is a hard name to pronounce, even in my own language, and I have never cared for it much, so you can give me whatever name you wish, I'll answer to that."

Aric frowned slightly. "A man should never be ashamed of his own name, but I will respect your wishes, as you are a guest in our house."

Turning to his wife, he winked, "Well, my dear, what shall we name our new arrival?"

Lauria thought for a moment, then spoke, "Well, how about Amar? My father always planned to name his first son Amar, but his wife only bore him daughters. You can be Amar, my brother."

I bobbed my head in a polite bow, "I would be most honored, thank you."

"So, Amar," Aric began, trying out the new name like one would taste a pie. "If you would like to follow me, we can wash the dust from our hands and have some dinner. May I just say that you are in for a treat, Lauria is the best cook in the village."

"My husband likes to exaggerate, Amar, you'll have to get used to him." Lauria said, but she could not suppress a pleased smile that spread across her face at his compliment.

I followed Aric to a well in the back of his house. A bucket sat by the well, but it looked old and untouched, grass growing around its edges. Rather than reach for the bucket and rope, Aric turned a hand crank vigorously and water came flowing from a spout into a trough. Aric stood back, looking proud of himself.

"Very nice." I probed, not sure yet what I was complimenting.

"Thank you, I invented it myself. The others in the village haven't started using it yet; they are still stuck in their old ways. They still choose to use a bucket for the wells in the village rather than my pump. I'm glad you appreciate it."

I leaned in to take a closer look at the pumping device, if he truly had invented it, than he was a clever craftsman indeed. The design was quite clever. A rod descended down into the murky depths of the well. Wound around the rod was a tube with a series of valves placed strategically so that the water would not flow back down into the well whenever some stopped turning the hand crank. When the crank was turned, a series of gears would spin the tube extremely fast and the water would be forced up through the tube from the reservoir below. At the top of the rod, the water would be flung out of the tube and caught in a small box that surrounded the top part of the tube and channeled the water through the spout.

"Do they use buckets where you come from?" Aric asked.

"Yes, a lot like here."

Aric looked torn between being flattered at truly being the first at something, and being disappointed that I had not brought news of a more advanced and free-thinking civilization.

When we went back into the house, hands washed, Lauria already had the table set with dinner. The fare was truly well made, though nothing fancy. To hear Aric talk about it after the meal, however, one would have thought that he had gained access to paradise and had just feasted on ambrosia. Lauria scolded him for his obvious exaggeration, smiling the whole time. Their banter quieted and I took the opportunity to start learning about their situation.

"So," I began, "that wall must have taken a very long time to build, I have never seen anything quite like it."

Aric nodded solemnly, "It was indeed a great project. We spend our youth hearing stories about it. I helped repair a small portion of it when I was an apprentice, and my father spent most of his youth working on the southern portion when an earthquake shook down a section of the wall. Destroyers had never been seen that far south, but it doesn't hurt to be careful. It's still not really enough, though."

I couldn't have asked for a more perfect opening.

"Oh? The Destroyers can still get through that wall?" I still didn't know who the Destroyers were, but this was a good way to start learning.

"Yes, they are very cunning. They come to attack and to steal our food and tools, leaving us with nothing to eat and nothing with which to work the land." Aric's troubled expression turned into a weary smile as he reached across the table to hold his wife's hand and continued.

"But, we are the Creators, we can rebuild faster than they can steal from us."

"The tragedy is when they take something from us that we cannot replace." Lauria added, her head bowed. Aric nodded, his countenance falling.

11

"There is scarcely anyone in the border villages who hasn't lost someone close to them to the Destroyer raids. I lost a good friend, and Lauria's father was killed by a Destroyer." Aric's gaze was sad. "We are not warriors, even one Destroyer is capable of inflicting great harm on us before we can muster sufficient numbers to defeat them or scare them off."

"Why haven't any of you trained how to fight better?" I asked, digging deeper.

"That is exactly what I have been suggesting for years, but it seems that what our people lack in skill, they make up for in cowardice.

"If a man knows how to fight, he is expected to, even before others. Every one of our villagers would rather be unskilled and a member of a mob than a warrior standing alone. That is the real reason.

"When asked about it, however, they will piously talk about how that is not our way and we would lose something of ourselves if we fought."

I could hear the contempt and frustration in his voice as he continued,

"I'm not even saying that that isn't a good reason, I only wish it were true. The truth of the matter is that we fight anyway, we just fight badly.

"As I said, we are not warriors."

Lauria seemed very anxious to change the subject. I wondered if it was more to keep Aric's mood from turning sour or to keep his slowly tightening hand from crushing hers. Her eyes raced for something to take note of, they landed on my feet.

"Don't they wear shoes where you come from?"

"Oh they do," I responded. "I just like to feel the land under me."

"You told me you were robbed." Aric interrupted.

"So I was, but I wasn't wearing shoes before that, they just took my pack and provisions." I wouldn't have been much of a Historian if I couldn't keep my lies straight.

"So, tell me about your land, what are your people like?" Lauria pressed on, keeping the focus on me.

Aric sat up straighter in his seat, anxious to listen. He was relaxed again, Lauria's small hand was safe.

"Oh, I'm afraid there really isn't much to tell. My people are truly a lot like yours, only we don't have Stones like yours. But then, we also don't have Destroyers or a great wall to keep them out."

"Hmm, that must be so wonderful, so peaceful." Lauria commented.

"Oh, I don't know about that." I smiled, "I think you would find that if your people didn't have the Destroyers to fight, they would soon find another battle, possibly among themselves. People can unite through many trials, but not for peace."

Aric sighed, "I suppose that you are right, Amar. I certainly have seen rifts among our own people that would erupt if we didn't have the threat of the Destroyers hanging over our heads. Has there been trouble among your people then? Is that perhaps one of the reasons you left?"

"No, no, I left merely because of my itching feet. I just can't seem to be satisfied with what's right in front of me." I replied.

Aric opened his mouth to ask more questions, but Lauria stopped him.

"Aric, our guest must be very weary from the road; perhaps we should all get some sleep."

Again, Aric bobbed his head in shame. "Oh yes, I'm so sorry Amar, I have again forgotten my manners. I hope that you will forgive me. If you don't mind, I'll set up a place for you out in my old shed. It might be a little small, but it is warm and it is private. I have built myself a new workshop, so I no longer have any need of it, so you're free to stay as long as you'd like."

I replied that that would be just fine and Aric led the way out the back of the house to a shed.

Lauria followed in due time and soon the shed was furnished with a makeshift bed, blankets, and even a pitcher of cool water, should I become thirsty. I doubted that I would have received this sort of hospitality at any other home in the village. They wished me goodnight and headed back to the house.

When their lights turned off, I quietly rose from my bed and went for a walk through the village. Each house, each corner, seemed a work of art, crafted by caring hands. A few people were still on the streets, mostly heading home. When they saw me, they crossed to the far side of the street and scuttled home as fast as they could. They knew I was under Aric's protection and guard, but they weren't about to take any unnecessary risks.

Part of me said that I should just leave this place; it was just like the many other towns I had traveled through. The people would be the same, the problems the same, there was nothing to see here. However, I still felt a curiosity about the wall, the Stones, and the Destroyers. More than that, an ancient instinct suggested that there might be a story here after all. Resolving to stay, I turned back towards Aric's shed and waited until morning.

Chapter 2

I can imagine no greater heroism than motherhood.
　　　　　　　　　　　　　　−Musings of the Historian

When Aric came out to wake me for breakfast, he had lines creasing his face and dark bags under his eyes; it didn't seem like he had slept much. His smile was as broad as ever as he greeted me.

"Obviously an early riser, Amar, good for you. However, you still haven't beat Lauria, breakfast is ready and on the table, so you had better come in quickly."

The breakfast was simple, a far cry from the great cooking that I had eaten the night before, mostly just cheese and bread. Lauria was nowhere to be seen. Aric was clearly distracted by something. On the one hand, I was glad that he wasn't asking me more questions about my past; but on the other hand, I wondered if his distraction had anything to do with Lauria. When I asked about her, Aric just shrugged his massive shoulders.

"She had some errands to run; she said that she would see you later, though. Go ahead and eat up."

After countless years of talking with people, it wasn't hard to tell when someone wasn't telling me the whole truth. Beyond that, Aric was a horrible liar. I wondered if Lauria was all right.

"Tell me, Aric, when is Lauria expected to have her baby?" I tested. It was a shot in the dark, but it hit dead center.

Aric smiled through his bloodshot eyes, "You are a sly one, Amar. She is going to have it very soon. In fact, she may be having it right now. I only tell you this because you are my guest, but it is considered bad luck in our culture to speak of such things as they are happening." Aric paused and smiled again, "In fact, the men are pretty much forbidden to interfere at all, or even take notice."

Aric paused, lowering his voice and leaning in closer, as if sharing a secret.

"Between you and me, I think it is one of the dumbest superstitions we have. How am I supposed to not worry about my wife?"

I opened my mouth to speak, but he answered his own question before I could get anything out, slamming his hand down on the table with a thundering clap.

"I work! That's how. Come with me, it's time to occupy my hands, you can help with the bellows." His chair almost fell over as he stood up quickly, knocking it backwards. I hurried to keep up as he walked out to his workshop in quick strides.

A fire was roaring in no time and Aric was soon pounding, almost recklessly, on a helpless piece of metal. He would pound for a while, then stick it back into the furnace as I worked the bellows, then pull it out and pound at it some more. I was fascinated to watch as he worked the metal. His fluid movements belied great experience, but the part that truly caught my eye was the Stone he wore around his neck. As he worked the metal, the Stone would glow with its own light from within as the glare from the furnace danced on its surface. It grew brighter as Aric made more and more specific modifications, sharpening edges and adding decorations to what now appeared to be a trowel head of some sort. I blinked to clear my eyes as I saw the Stone glow even brighter when Aric worked in some intricate detail. The decoration was obviously unnecessary, it was just a simple farm tool, but Aric worked at it with a burning intensity. He apparently didn't have a complex job to do that day, so he would make a complex job out of a simple one.

I wondered more and more about the Stone around Aric's neck as it continued to throb and glow brighter as the metal was shaped under Aric's expert hand.

This would explain the great workmanship that I had seen along the wall and in the town. If Aric could create this sort of workmanship with his Stone, certainly there were others equally as skilled in working wood, stone, or anything else. I yelled over the clanging and the furnace to Aric.

"Does the color of your Stone determine your expertise?"

Aric looked confused for a moment, and then nodded, sweat dripping from his forehead, still focused on adding meaningless decoration to the trowel.

"The blues have always been metal workers, that is our gift from the Stones. Others have different gifts." Aric spoke without breaking from his task, the hammer continuing to fall in steady strokes. The hammer seemed almost an extension of his arm, the power flowing smoothly from his shoulders, down his arm, through the hammer, and into the metal.

"Greens, for instance, have always had a special gift over plants, trees, and other such living things. You may have noticed Lauria's stone."

I nodded. "Light blue."

"Light blues have always been the stone cutters and

shapers. I make enough with my shop so that she does not have to work, but most of the plates and other dishes in our home were made by her."

The pride in his voice was obvious, and for good reason. I had noticed the plates the night before and at breakfast. At first I had thought that they had brought out special dishes in my honor, but a quick glance around the house showed that every other dish displayed the same intricacy in its design.

"What about the red Stones?" I asked. "I noticed that the man who wanted me dead wore one."

Aric nodded grimly and pounded a bit harder at the glowing metal. "Yes, Saddhan, he is a cruel man. As near as we can tell, the red Stones give their owners special skills with fire. Unfortunately, there is no great craft in fires, so they spend most of their time as merchants. Some, like Saddhan, set themselves up as leaders over the people. He owns a shop in town, but he doesn't spend much time there."

"How does he make money, then?" I asked.

"Well, there's a tax that's collected from all of the people. It was originally Saddhan's idea. The wall kept the Destroyers away for a very long time; but when they started finding ways to get over the wall, Saddhan insisted that we needed to post lookouts and guards."

Aric spat, "Guards. A fat lot of good they do. They are supported by our money, but they are widespread and lazy. You notice that we knew nothing of your coming until you were practically walking down our street."

I nodded, I had seen no guards, and I had walked for a long time.

18

"So," Aric continued. "Saddhan has declared himself captain of the guards and guardian of our safety."

Contempt dripped from every syllable as Aric spoke about the man.

"Near as I can tell, all that he does is take long walks; patrols, he calls them, and gets fat off of the money he takes from…"

Aric's head suddenly shot up, his hands trembling. Suddenly he dropped both his hammer and the piece he was working on and tore out of the workshop. I ran after him. In a few moments, I also heard what he had been listening for: cheering.

Chapter 3

There are few things more powerful than a name. A single phrase that somehow becomes a symbol for an entire existence. What can it mean that mine is gone?

–Musings of the Historian

A young boy had obviously been sent running to get Aric, because he met us halfway, breathless.

"Boy!" The lad managed to yell out breathlessly as Aric drew near, "It's a boy."

Aric was to him in seconds, grabbing the youth by the shoulders and lifting him off the ground to eye level.

"And Lauria? Is she all right?" Aric asked frantically.

The boy nodded, "She's fine, she's with the midwife now."

Aric dropped the boy unceremoniously on the ground and ran on through the town. I glanced back at the boy who had been dropped. He didn't look at all surprised by Aric's conduct. He mostly seemed glad to be able to rest and rub his shoulders where Aric had gripped them.

We ran into a group of people who were gathered around a building that I guessed was the midwife's house. Several people slapped Aric on the back and repeated the news that the breathless lad had already delivered; a son had been born and Lauria was doing just fine. Aric, after catching his breath, asked.

"What color of Stone was he born with?"

Some of the people started to look confused, as if they hadn't thought of that before. One woman spoke up.

"That's odd, Aric, the midwife didn't say, she only yelled that it was a boy."

Murmurs spread through the crowd. I gathered that the color of a child's Stone was usually announced with his birth. Aric's joy couldn't be dimmed, however, he just shrugged his shoulders and laughed.

"That would be my son, all right, even distracted the midwife, cute little devil."

Everyone laughed at Aric's lightheaded wit.

A stern looking woman poked her head out the window and ordered Aric into the house. He quickly complied.

I was shocked to see Aric emerge a few minutes later with the baby in his arms and Lauria, looking exhausted but still smiling by his side, leaning heavily on his broad arm. I had seen a great many births, and it was almost always a long time, sometimes even days, before the woman was allowed to walk about or the baby was strong enough to be taken home. In this case, both mother and child seemed healthy, although completely exhausted. I wondered if it had anything to do with the Stones that the people wore. Maybe there was one that helped the midwife to speed recovery, or perhaps these women were naturally very hardy. I wasn't excluding any possibilities just yet.

Aric pushed his way through the cheering crowd. Some in the crowd asked what color the baby's Stone was, but Aric seemed not to hear them, entirely engrossed in his new child. The crowd slowly dissipated, respecting the couple's privacy and the sacred moment of taking the child home. I followed at a distance.

Only one man followed closely, Saddhan. He wore a look of deep suspicion and seemed intent on satisfying his curiosity at any cost. I was surprised at his audacity as he entered the house after them and closed the door behind him. I waited outside the door and listened to the voices within.

"What color is the baby's Stone, Aric? What are you trying to hide?" Saddhan's tone was accusing.

"One moment, you old woman, let me put my wife to bed first, then I will listen to your cackling." Aric's voice, which had been so gleeful only minutes before on the street, had developed a bitter edge.

There was a long silence as Saddhan waited in the living room and I waited outside the door for Aric to put Lauria to bed with the baby. Aric's heavy footsteps again sounded on the floor and Saddhan's high-pitched voice again demanded.

"Well?"

"You want to see my baby's Stone, Saddhan, then you will, but know that it means nothing."

I heard a gasp from Saddhan and I knew that something was wrong. It only took a couple of seconds before Saddhan's screeches broke the awkward silence.

"It is one of the Destroyers! No light passes through the Stone!" Saddhan's loud ravings reached the entire village and people were already starting to filter back onto the streets to see what was going on.

"The child must be killed, Aric! You know the law! We can't have that... that THING living among us! Hey now, you just stay back. Why are you protecting it anyway? Think of what this child means." Saddhan's voice lowered slightly, I had to lean closer to the door to hear.

"Maybe your precious little Lauria hasn't been quite so faithful as you thought."

I stepped quickly to the side, away from the door. My hunch paid off as Saddhan was thrown through the door, the wood splintering as his weight crashed through it. He landed hard and rolled in the dust. Aric came through the door after him, looking like a Titan ready to pull the heavens down on top of the quivering man. His face was red and the veins in his arms bulged as he pointed at Saddhan and bellowed in a voice that reverberated through the watching crowd.

"If you ever speak another word like that I will rip your head from your shoulders, Saddhan! I will not allow your bitterness to taint my home. The boy is my son and he will be raised as such."

Aric raised his eyes to the crowd who stood with jaws gaping wide in surprise.

"This is my child's Stone!" Aric yelled and lifted his hand high to show the people its contents. The Stone, unlike the clear Stones of the villagers, was opaque. Beyond that, it was of no color at all, but of the deepest black, and it almost seemed to draw light from around it, making its surroundings seem darker. The people drew back in fear, as if they expected the Stone itself to attack them. In a single instant, the observant crowd of about thirty people had become a mob, a creature of impulse and rage.

"It is the Stone of a Destroyer!"

"It's evil!"

"The child should be destroyed!"

"The law must be obeyed!"

The shouts from the mob turned from confusion to anger in a moment. These were frightened people, and frightened people were dangerous. Saddhan had crawled to the back of the crowd, gasping and holding his arm, and soon his voice added to the angry din. Aric stood his ground and roared back at them like a lion defending his cub.

"He will not be killed!"

The crowd didn't lose a second in answering.

"It's the law!"

"Then it will be disobeyed!" Came the thundering response. The mob would not be dissuaded, however.

"Then what will you do with him?"

"He will stay with us."

"No! He can't!" The tone of the crowd had already turned desperate and dangerous.

"Why not?" Aric questioned, but his voice had already taken on the tone of one who knew that words weren't going to do any good. Standing to the side, I could clearly see his fist clench at his side, the thick cords of muscle in his arm tightening. His words were only meant to delay what was surely coming.

Out of the crowd stepped an older man, this one with a far calmer look on his face. His graying hair and sad eyes spoke of wisdom. A red Stone hung about his neck. Judging by the way he held himself and how the people deferred to him, I would guess that this was a leader among this people. Speaking softly, his voice cut through the yelling.

"Aric, we understand that you don't want to get rid of your child, any of us would feel the same. You must remember that these things have happened before, but we must not shrink away from our responsibility. Besides, how will your son fit in among us, what will he do without a craft? Maybe it would be better if we turned him over to the Destroyers when he is old enough to be away from his mother."

Aric started to object, but was beaten to it by the wild objections of the villagers.

"To what end, Boran? He will only grow to come back over here and kill us and steal our food."

Boran, the older man, tried to quiet the crowd, but with little success. Aric, in the meantime, had suddenly become very thoughtful. Suddenly his head rose.

"He will fight for us!" Aric yelled decisively. The crowd quieted, awaiting further explanation.

"We all know that one Destroyer is worth five of our best men in a fight, and we all have lost loved ones to their raids. I will raise my boy to be a fighter; he will stand against them and protect us. He will be a warrior, that will be his craft!"

The mob shifted, mulling amongst themselves. The idea had merit. Their cowardice and the appeal of having someone else fight their battles for them was being weighed against their hatred and suspicion.

Aric moved to tip the scales. He eased open the door and ducked inside it for just a moment before reappearing with one of his blacksmith hammers held in his meaty fist. The hammer bore the scars of thousands of strokes. The head was large and heavy, but Aric held it lightly, as if it weighed no more than a stick.

"That is what will happen, I will say no more. If any of you persist in wanting to harm my family, I will consider you worse than the Destroyers and I will be waiting inside for you. I bid you all a good day."

Aric raised the hammer in a parting salute, turned and
started to walk back into the house. Almost as an afterthought, he
turned and said:

"His name will be Sadavir."

With that, Aric turned and walked back inside. I would
have said that the door wouldn't close with its damaged hinges,
having nearly been knocked into the street by Saddhan's thrown
body, but a strong pull by Aric's arm shifted the door into its
place. A momentary silence fell on the street.

"Well, let's get him! He can't fight all of us!" The high-
pitched scream was unmistakable. Saddhan's demand, however,
only served to solidify the reality of Aric's threat in the minds of
the mob. They shifted slightly, then scattered like dry leaves tossed
by an autumn wind. With the mob dissolved, Saddhan skulked
away, limping and holding his arm.

The cowardice that Aric had mocked the night before had
at last served a useful purpose.

Chapter 4

Great language and great literature do not survive long without each other.

–Musings of the Historian

In the days that followed, things settled into an uneasy peace. When I was sent into town after something, I was shunned outright. I hadn't really expected anything different. What did surprise me was one time when I watched Lauria go into town to buy some cloth. They treated her in much the same way as they treated me, like an outsider.

Aric mostly kept to himself in his shop. One day, while working the bellows, I tried to get Aric to talk about it.

"So, Aric, when I first came into town, you were working out in the fields with the other villagers. Does that not happen anymore? I see others go."

Aric looked toward the village.

"Most of the actual tending of plants is left to the ones with green Stones, but often more help is needed and they will call on us to go out and help them plow, weed, harvest, or whatever they need done. We all try to pitch in as much as we can, food is necessary for all of us." He replied.

"And there is no need of such help now, Aric?" I pried. Aric set his hammer down and looked up at me.

"I think you already know the answer to that question.

There is always help needed in some field or another. But the ways things work, someone comes around and invites people to go out and work. No one comes to this house any more."

"Why not just go out and help anyway?" I asked.

"And have them glare at me out of the corners of their eyes? Just to listen to the silence, perhaps? I know when I am not wanted, Amar. I won't force the issue, that would only make it worse."

"Maybe."

"Do you think there's another way, Amar? Do you think I should be crawling to those would-be child killers?" Aric asked, the half-done door hinge cooling into blackness behind him as he turned on me.

"Now, Aric, you know that I would never even suggest that. What they did was wrong, that's for sure. But the choice of how to deal with it is yours, Aric, it will always be yours."

Aric nodded, resigned. "Yes, Amar, I know. But it's not just their anger toward me that I'm fighting here. I am also fighting my own anger towards them. Do you think I don't see the way they look at my wife when she goes into town? Do you think I don't see her tears in the night as those who were her friends abandon her? How can I forgive them if they won't accept us or even seek our forgiveness?

"Your words are wise, Amar, but I still don't know what it is you're telling me to do."

"I'm not telling you to do anything, Aric. That is not my role here. I am warning you about letting the actions of others decide your feelings and your fate."

Aric said nothing in response. He turned back to his work.

28

The next day, he came to me and requested that I walk with him.

"Lauria needs some more thread, I'm going to get it. Would you like to come?"

I nodded, realizing his intentions. He would no longer submit Lauria to the glares of the villagers, he would go himself.

I kept pace beside him as his giant steps sped him to the center of town. Villagers, seeing us coming, crossed to the other side of the road. Aric nodded to them respectfully. Their eyes darted away as they pretended not to have noticed. Aric was not to be deterred, however, and he continued to nod and even wave at every person he saw.

Without exception, he was ignored. They didn't remember the friend that Aric had been to them. These people held grudges and they were good at it. The reaction at the local traders was much the same. He supplied the thread without even so much as a hello or a thank you as he coolly accepted the money that Aric offered.

Aric walked mechanically out of the store and back toward his home. A rock struck him in the back and he whipped around to see who had thrown it. There were too many people on the street to identify the culprit. My eyes caught Padam, Saddhan's five-year old son, dart behind a building. Aric turned back and continued his walk toward his home. Soon, another rock hit him in the back. This time, Aric did not even respond, but continued his weary trudge back to his house.

Reaching his house, he handed Lauria the thread, not responding to her questioning gaze. He walked out the back of the house and in no time at all, the sound of his ringing hammer could be heard.

The following days were much the same. Aric persisted in living as he always had, and the villagers persisted in ignoring him. I doubt that my presence in his home helped much, but he didn't seem to mind. In fact, he seemed quite grateful to have someone to work the bellows for him, especially when all I asked in return was the use of his old shed.

Sadavir, for his part, grew very rapidly, and even as a very small boy, showed incredible quickness and intelligence. It was all that Lauria could do to keep him out of the sugar. It didn't matter how high up on a shelf she put it, it was never out of reach for Sadavir. Aric was sitting on a chair watching Sadavir as he unashamedly put together a makeshift ladder of chairs and a mixing bowl to reach up to the dish shelf, where Lauria had tried to hide the sugar bowl from him.

"Aric?" I tested.

"Yes, Amar?"

"What were the people talking about when they were talking about the law you were breaking?"

Aric sighed. "It happens very rarely, but sometimes a child is born with a Destroyer's Stone."

"And...?" I prompted after he didn't continue.

"It's simple to them, Amar, any and all Destroyers can't live among us."

"So are they banished when they're older?"

"You already know what they intended when they came to this house, Amar. The children never grow old enough to be banished. They are killed at birth, their Stones crushed."

"And who does this?" I asked, horrified at discovering infanticide practiced among these peaceful people.

"The father does it. I broke the law when I left the midwife's house."

I was flabbergasted. "You were supposed to murder your own child right there in the house?!"

He nodded. "That's one of the reasons the husband isn't supposed to take notice of the birth, he should not get excited about the child coming until he knows whether he will be father or executioner that day."

"How is it done?" I asked.

"To tell you the truth, Amar, I don't quite know. This is only the second time in my lifetime that such a thing has happened in this village. The midwife started to explain; I pushed her into a chair, took my wife and child and left. If Lauria wasn't so strong, it might have endangered her life to take her out so soon. As for Sadavir, he seemed to be strong from the very beginning."

One more mystery solved, I thought to myself. Aric didn't seem to be annoyed at my questioning, so I decided to investigate further.

"Are all Destroyers' Stones black?" I asked.

"No, in color, they are much like ours. I have never seen a black one." Aric admitted.

"They also have their blues, greens, reds, and so on. The difference is that their Stones let no light pass through them, you can see no deeper than the surface."

Clear or opaque, it seemed like such a small thing to create such a rift between people. But then, people never needed much of an excuse to set one person, or groups of people, below themselves. It was human nature. For one person to be better, one had to be worse.

"So if they also have their specialties, why can't they build their own tools instead of stealing yours?" I queried.

Aric looked puzzled. "I forget that you do not have Stones where you come from, Amar. They cannot make their own because they are the Destroyers. Our Stones add to the form and beauty of the materials we work with. Their Stones have only the power to dismantle, to obscure. That is why we call them the Destroyers, they even call themselves Destroyers."

"Wait a moment," I interrupted. "How do you know what they call themselves, Aric?"

"Well, we've wounded them before, and before the men finished them off, they yelled at us. Mostly they just insulted us, calling us 'Creator dogs' or things similar to it. But a couple of them have pleaded the cause of their people before they died. Usually they only get out something like 'have pity on the Destroyers' or something like that before one of Saddhan's men silence them forever."

"So how did you understand them? Do you understand their language?"

"Actually, Amar, they speak ours. Or we started out speaking theirs, that part is a little confusing, but the fact remains that we speak the same language."

"How is that possible?" I asked, confused. People who were separated even for short periods of time tended to develop their own dialects and even languages. From what I had heard from Aric, these people had been separated for as long as anyone could remember.

"Hmm, to tell you the truth, Amar, I hadn't really thought about it. No one really knows. I would assume that if the people once lived together, they would keep the same language. They do speak with a bit of an accent." He offered.

"How do you keep your language from changing?" I pressed. Aric looked confused at the question. I rephrased it.

"What I mean is, how do you make sure that other villages don't start speaking a little differently? If two people use different words, how would you know which one is right?"

"Oh, I understand what you're asking now. Our children are taught from the book. The book is our standard, so I guess that's how we haven't changed our language."

"I haven't seen any books around, where do you keep them?" I asked, maybe a little too eagerly. If anything would shed some light on these people and their past, it would be the books that they had written.

"Well, the teacher for the village keeps it at his house, the children go to him to be taught when they are eight years old. They study with him until they are ten, then they start their apprenticeship with whatever master takes them in.

"Sometimes, parents will have their children go back to school a few years later if they didn't learn well enough during the first two years. Of course, they have to have the permission of whichever master the child is studying with. In Sadavir's case, since there are no masters with black Stones, I will be his master.

"I was going to be taking on a promising young lad with a blue Stone from the village, but his parents have already spoken to me. It appears that they've found someone else." The disappointment in his voice was obvious. I had seen the work of some of the other blacksmiths in town. Aric was, by far, the best of all of them. His ingenuity added an original tone to his work. It was a testament to his skill that even though they wanted nothing to do with him personally, he still received a steady supply of orders for his metalwork.

Any craftsman of that caliber would want his legacy passed on. It was clear that Sadavir would never be a blacksmith, and now it was becoming clear that he would have no other apprentices. His art would die with him.

About then, Lauria came back in, shooting Aric a dirty look for simply looking on as his only son stole the sugar. She moved to intervene as Aric bobbed his head in the direction of the door as he stood up. I followed him out onto his small front porch. He sat down on the edge of it and I sat down next to him, a new question burning in my mind.

"Now, Aric, when you talked about books, you just said 'it.' Are you really saying that there is only one book?"

Aric looked puzzled. "How many could there be?"

Chapter 5

This one thing I can promise you: You don't know a blasted thing about the nature of reality.

–Musings of the Historian

I didn't know how to respond to that.

"Umm, never mind, Aric. I guess what I really want to know is, what is in that book?"

"Mostly, it is a recounting of our early history, when the Destroyers attacked us and we threw them back into their own land and built the wall. Frankly, it sounds as if someone like Saddhan wrote it. It depicts the Destroyers as a disease that we successfully cured."

"What about since then, are there any histories about the time since then?"

Aric was puzzled again. "I would like to visit your land, sometime, Amar. Here, the book is to teach our children why they must fear the Destroyers and to make sure that they learn how to speak correctly. What else could there be?"

Again I was at a loss for words; a society without literature. Their school sounded like little more than a speech class centered on brainwashing.

"Would it be possible for me to see this book?" I asked.

Aric shook his head. "It is kept with the teacher. If our book were to be destroyed, it would take a very long time for our teacher to go to another village and copy down the symbols from their book. So, the book is never given to anyone else.

"However, if you are truly interested in hearing what it says, I'm sure we can arrange something. When they are teaching, the parents are free to stay around and listen. Usually, it's just for overly protective parents who don't want to leave their children. Some just enjoy the stories. You could go in my place and watch over Sadavir for me and then you could hear the book as it is taught to the children."

I nodded. "I would like that very much."

Something else occurred to me.

"Aric, do you think it's possible that the Destroyers also have a copy of the book and that they teach their children in much the same way?"

"Frankly, Amar, I don't know." Aric shrugged. "We don't actually know much about how they live on the far side of the wall. Even before the wall was built, our people avoided theirs, so we only see them when they raid us. Most people believe that they are like animals; that they run around, killing and eating whatever they can catch or steal. To the minds of most of my people, they are little more than dogs."

"What do you think, Aric?"

"Well," Aric spoke hesitantly. "Animals have no real need to dress themselves, these men do. Animals have no need to speak, these men do. Also, if they were just animals, then I think that we would have seen women also attack. As it is, we have only ever seen men get past the wall to attack us. I think they protect their women, just as we do." Aric's voice had dropped to almost a whisper, as if he were afraid of someone overhearing.

"Also," He continued. "They have often stolen tools from us, but I have never seen them use those tools against us as weapons, they use their own weapons for that. So I think it's possible that they might be like us. I think they farm, or at least try to. I think that they work with metal, but they don't have the help of the Stones. If anything, their Stones would impede their progress."

"Do you hate them, Aric?" I spoke softly.

Aric's shoulders dropped slightly. "I know I should, Amar. Everyone else does. They hurt us and they have killed people very close to me. I certainly have every reason to hate them."

Aric fell silent for a moment.

"But...?" I prompted.

"But I can't help but think that if I didn't have any way to get food or to farm, and if my wife and son were starving, if it were my Lauria and my Sadavir, then I would do whatever it took to provide for them. I would even risk my life getting over a dangerous wall and attacking people who had what I needed."

Aric finished and his head bowed.

"And yet you will raise Sadavir to fight them?" I asked.

Aric's head raised and he looked me straight in the eye.

"Yes, Amar, I will. I understand what would drive them to do what they do, but I still can't let them do it. These are still my people. My Lauria and my Sadavir are on this side of the wall, so my loyalties lie here. Do you think me wrong?"

At his last question, Aric's voice had taken on a sharp edge. I laughed softly to lighten the mood.

"No, my large friend, I would do the same in your place. Furthermore, I think that you are a good man for trying to understand your enemy, very few try. Just be sure you teach

Sadavir to think the same. A warrior who hates his enemy will soon become like them."

Another silence fell, Aric was looking into the distance as if trying to catch some glimpse of the wisdom and strength he would need to properly raise his child. I again broke into his reverie.

"Aric, you have already stated your intention to raise your boy as a warrior. How do you intend to do that? After all, no one here knows very much about fighting. How can a peaceful man teach war?"

"Ah, Amar, you have a sharp mind, you never fail to cut right to the heart of the matter. I have been thinking about that quite a lot."

Aric suddenly perked up, "You wouldn't know anything about it, would you?" He asked hopefully.

"I'm afraid not, I'm just a wanderer, not a warrior." I replied. Aric resumed his original pose of thoughtfulness.

"Well then, lacking any help, I think I will let him learn on his own. I will merely ensure that he grows up strong. Then I will give him plenty of opportunities to figure out how to defend himself; and to strike back, if need be." Aric shrugged his shoulders apologetically. "I'm afraid it's the only plan I have. The Destroyers have learned how to fight on their own, no one had to teach them."

"Well, judging from how the Stones have been able to help you surpass your natural abilities, maybe that is the best plan there is for raising a Destroyer." I instantly regretted my use of the title as I saw Aric's brow tighten into a scowl.

"He isn't a Destroyer, Amar. He may carry the Stone, but in

his heart he is still my son, I am sure of it." Aric said.

"I'm sure he is." I responded, not wanting to cause any more trouble for myself or anxiety for him.

"Now Amar," Aric started, his expression changing from troubled to the same look of eager curiosity I had seen the first day I had met him. "You have been asking a great many questions and finding out everything about us while I've sat here like a big talking head. That has gone on for far too long. The day has come that you're going to sit there and answer some of my questions."

It hadn't been a question, and I was certain that if I tried to duck out of it this time, I would likely be physically restrained.

"Very well, Aric, let's hear your questions, but understand that there are some questions that I will not answer."

Aric considered this for a moment, then nodded and launched into his questions.

"First, Amar, what is your name, your true name? I don't care if I can't pronounce it, I would like to know your name."

"I've forgotten it, Aric."

"What?" Aric looked at me, disgusted. "A man doesn't forget his own name, Amar. Come then, out with it."

"Honestly, Aric, I can't tell you my name. When I came here, you gave me a name, didn't you?"

"Yes…" Aric replied, not understanding my point.

"Well, just as this name was given to me, my true name was taken by someone else. I hope one day they will give it back to me. Until then, I don't have a name, except the one you've given me. You call me Amar, and so I am."

Aric stared at me. "Amar, without a doubt, that is the craziest thing I have ever heard. But I guess I'll have to pass on that question. Next question, where are you from?"

"I am from Surac."

"So your land is also named… wait. Amar, the next time you answer one of my questions like that, I swear I'm going to knock you flat on your back, so help me." Aric raised his massive fist to back up his threat.

I smiled again. "Aric, trust me, I'm not being flippant. I don't have a home any more than I have a name."

"Fine, I'll ask a simpler question. Where were you before you came to Surac? And I'm warning you, if you say 'walking through the country,' you'll be getting no dinner tonight."

"I came from a place where everything was made of metal and stone for as far as the eye could see. Energy like lightning from a summer storm pulsed through everything and made the entire land alive. And men could live forever."

"Uhh…" Aric started, then trailed off, his jaw hanging open as he stared at me and wondered what to think about what I had said and whether or not to believe me. Finally, he spoke in a low whisper, leaning forward slightly to look directly into my eyes, searching.

"Amar, would you make up a story like that? Is there truly a land like that?"

I nodded. Aric continued in his low whisper of awed curiosity.

"How long would it take me to walk there?"

"Longer than you will live, Aric, and then some. Besides, the people there don't walk, they are carried from place to place by metal inventions that don't touch the ground."

I toyed with the idea of putting a rock into Aric's gaping

mouth. I don't think he would have noticed.

"Why did you leave?" Aric asked, once he could speak again after receiving this latest tidbit of information.

"The story was over."

Aric's awed look changed to one of confusion.

"What do you mean, the story was over?"

"I only stay as long as there is a story to be witnessed."

Aric nodded, his eyes blank. He hadn't truly understood; his mind was back in the strange land I had told him about. An idea occurred to him.

"You went there, and you made it here. Why couldn't I go back the same way? I'm sure they wouldn't worry about Sadavir's Stone in a place like that."

"I'm sure they wouldn't, Aric, but that place doesn't exist anymore."

"What?" Aric looked as though he might cry. He had already been struggling with the idea that such a land could even exist. To bring up going there had been a grasping at straws that revealed his innermost desperation. "What could happen to a land as mighty as that?"

"The entire land was consumed in the blink of an eye by a fire, thousands of times hotter than the hottest fire in your forge. Their intelligent metal was turned from solid to liquid to gas to pure energy in less time than it takes you to swing a hammer."

Aric didn't respond, he just sat and stared into space for a while before standing up and walking back inside to dinner. Dinner was eaten in silence, Aric's food was herded from one side of his plate to the other and back again as Lauria stared at her life's companion. She looked at me questioningly, an eyebrow rose quizzically.

"These rolls are fantastic, Lauria." I offered, hiding my smile behind a long drink of water. Flashing me an angry look, she turned on her distracted husband.

"And how do you like the rolls, Aric?" She demanded.

"Oh, what?" Aric started like a man half asleep. "Oh, the rolls; yes, they're fantastic, darling." He mumbled, the roll on his plate completely untouched. His attention turned back to his plate and his potatoes started their migration back to the right side of his plate. Finally, his dinner uneaten, he retreated to the bedroom and curled up on his bed, awaiting unconsciousness. Lauria stood up from the table, crossed the room and closed the door on her troubled husband. She turned on me.

"What on earth were the two of you talking about out there?!" She demanded, her voice low and insistent.

"Oh, blacksmithing." I replied and got up from the table. As I walked out of the house to go to my shed, I was struck in the back of the head by a hard-thrown roll.

Chapter 6

A kind world would wait until children were old enough before exposing them to life's harsher truths. I have never walked a kind world.

-Musings of the Historian

The next morning, Aric was back to his normal, cheery self. After that night, Aric never spoke about leaving Surac. He had made up his mind to see this battle through to the end. Also, he didn't ask me any more questions about my past. Once, when Lauria started to ask me more about where I came from, he quickly shook his head at her and changed the subject. In my defense, I had hardly ever had anyone believe my stories of other lands, it had been a diversionary tactic. Somehow this blacksmith had known I was telling the truth.

Finally, all curiosity faded and I simply became Uncle Amar, a member of the family. The only remnant of our conversation was a look that Aric gave me occasionally that made it clear that he suspected I was more than what I appeared.

For the townspeople, it was quite the opposite. They never saw me as anything but an outsider. If anything, their suspicions and hatred grew as the little blacksmithing cottage came to be seen as a haven for the feared and unknown.

Sadavir was just learning to talk when his training began. I was fascinated to see the methods Aric used in training the boy.

He obviously had thought it out a great deal, far beyond the simplistic plan that he had shared with me. When the lad was four years old or so, well before his normal age of apprenticeship, his father presented him with a rock, about the size of my fist and smooth on all sides.

"Would you like to help me, Sadavir?"

The boy nodded eagerly.

"Ok then, this is a very special rock, a magical rock, it can't touch the ground or anything else. I can't carry it around with me during the day. I need to work. So I need you to carry it for me, can you do that?"

Sadavir nodded quickly, happy to be helping his father.

I was impressed by the dedication the boy showed to his task. In the days that followed, I never saw him without his rock, although I could see that he often became tired from carrying it. Every night, he would give the rock to his father, and every morning Aric would awaken the boy and hand him the rock for him to carry.

Sadavir incorporated the small burden into all of his usual chores and play, either learning to do things with one hand, or gripping the rock between his legs while he did something with both hands. I even saw him once walking back and forth in the house with it carefully balanced on his head. The rock had become part of his life. An odd pair indeed as the rock took the place of the friends the young boy should have had.

Still, there was no lack of love in the home. Being outcast from the village social scene, the small family grew even closer, drawing me into it. I'd never seen a child who had better parents than young Sadavir.

As time wore on and Sadavir grew, I noticed that the rock seemed to be growing right along with him. This I couldn't quite accept, so I confronted Aric about the changing rock.

In response, he took me to his shop and pulled back a small sheet that was behind his furnace. There lay several rocks, almost completely identical to the one Sadavir toted around with him, varying only slightly in size.

"Lauria makes them." He explained simply.

"Do you think that Sadavir suspects anything?"

"I expect he does, he is a very smart boy, but as long as he keeps carrying the rock, it doesn't much matter. He is growing strong under its weight. He is having to learn balance and ingenuity. As I told you, I know nothing of how men fight one another, but I can make sure he has the skills to not get hurt."

I was glad when Sadavir turned eight and I got to take him to the teacher's house for school. Although I'm afraid it wasn't such a great experience for Sadavir. My best guess was that the parents of the other kids had already told them about Sadavir and told them how to deal with him. He was an outcast the moment he stepped into the room. Some of the kids simply ignored him, some pointed and laughed at the rock Sadavir clutched firmly in his hands.

I saw Sadavir's hands tighten on the rock he held and his lips turn white as he clenched them together. Whether he was holding back tears or rage, I couldn't tell, but one thing was certain, he wasn't going to give the other children the satisfaction of a reaction. He walked forward and sat down cross-legged on one of the many mats that formed a semi-circle around the teacher's chair. He placed his rock in his lap and stared down at it, not wanting to look at anyone else. The other kids quickly moved mats around so as to be as far away from Sadavir as possible.

The teacher was a thin, wiry man. A rough complexion, combined with a spattering of short, rough hair on his almost bald head gave him the appearance of an old scrub brush. He saw the treatment of Sadavir clearly, but didn't interfere in the cruel actions of the students. If anything, I saw a faint smile flicker across his lips as he saw Sadavir alienated from his peers. The teacher took special care to let his gaze wander over to Sadavir each time he spoke about the Destroyers. The book he taught from gave him plenty of opportunities.

It took us a long time to get through even half the book, most of the year, in fact. The book and the story was used to illustrate examples of their writing system, a very fitting one for its purpose, which was truly little more than a speech lesson. They had a simple alphabet of phonetic symbols, which combined in patterns, one on top of another, to make words. There was no way of knowing which symbol came first in the word pattern, however, so the students ultimately just had to memorize what the different words looked like, the symbols just taught them which sounds made up each word.

All of the children learned very quickly. Sadavir, however, outshined them all as he picked up all of the symbols and words effortlessly. He had his mother's eyes and his father's keen mind.

He needed it too; the school required a lot of effort. Each day, the children spent six hours studying at the feet of their teacher. It wasn't long before the other parents stopped coming. Although I noticed that some left on the first day, right after they realized that I was going to attend.

The first five hours were spent purely on words and symbols. The teacher would show them in the book, then write it in the dust at his feet and instructed his students to follow along, although he seldom took much notice to see if they were actually doing it right. It didn't that the students long to pick up on this and the lazier ones were soon just scribbling nonsense. It wasn't long before Sadavir was the only one making a genuine effort to scrawl the correct symbols in the fine dust.

One day I noticed that he started sketching out the symbols for one word even before the teacher had started. The teacher reached down beside his chair and grabbed a stick that he kept there for disciplining the students. He rapped it down hard across Sadavir's hand. Sadavir jerked his hand back and held it, holding his breath to keep from crying.

"We all do this together, boy. You just love to show off, don't you? Do you think you're that much better than the other students?" He snapped.

Tears welled in Sadavir's eyes as he shook his head, not trusting his voice.

"Well, you act like it, you arrogant little pup." The teacher finished. Sadavir took special care after that to not start writing until after the teacher had started. But even then I noticed that he wasn't copying the teacher's lines in the dust, but rather what he remembered from the book. By the time six months had rolled by, Sadavir's writing was already better than the teacher's, a fact that the the old scrub brush of a man pointedly ignored.

After the five hours of instruction were over, the teacher would read over what they had covered for the day, making sure that the students heard the story they were studying.

"…The Destroyers came again in the daylight, while the men were out in the field. They killed several of the women and kidnapped several children as slaves. When the men returned to their burned homes, they vowed not to let the ravishing of the Destroyers touch their homes again. The men appointed some to stay home and keep watch, sounding the alarm if they should see any of the vicious creatures.

"But it still wasn't enough to stop the treachery of the Destroyers…"

The text related story after story of the Destroyers burning, looting and pillaging the villages of the peaceful Creators. When the text talked about the evil of the Destroyers, the teacher would look directly at Sadavir. For several months, Sadavir would look down at the dust under his feet, avoiding confrontation.

After a month or two, however, Sadavir would return the teacher's gaze coolly, refusing to be intimidated. I admired the lad's courage, few children of that age could even speak to an adult who wasn't a parent, much less defy them as Sadavir did.

The history was blatantly biased. What struck me though, was the simplistic style of the writing. For being the only book of the people, I had hoped that it would at least be a good literary work. I had even held out hope that it might be an epic poem. Instead, it was almost as if it had been written by a teenager complaining about the class bully. The book didn't even follow all of the grammatical rules the teacher taught the students.

The class still accepted it hook, line, and sinker. They especially enjoyed the stories. As the first year wore on, the mood of the class turned from distant to outright hostile toward Sadavir. At first, he tried to make reconciliations and make friends. It quickly became apparent that there wasn't a single kid in the class who would even speak to him. Most of the kids rallied around one child in tormenting Sadavir.

That child was Padam, Saddhan's son. He was much older than most of the other children in the class. He was obviously one of those who was reenrolled to better learn the history and symbols. It was clear just what kind of student he had been the first time around. Even the younger students had surpassed Padam after only a few months. Rather than trying harder to keep up with his peers, Padam would instruct them how to fool the teacher so they wouldn't have to work. Beyond that, Padam took it upon himself like a personal crusade to torment Sadavir.

Any time a child would treat Sadavir with the least degree of human kindness, it was certain that that child would get a visit from Padam. If he couldn't convince them by telling them how evil Destroyers were, he would simply resort to bullying and threats. Being about four years older than most of the students present, there weren't any of the students who would dare stand on Sadavir's side against Padam. In time, all the children found it much more fun to join in the crowd to mock Sadavir.

This carried on for about a year, roughly half of Sadavir's required time of schooling. At that time, Padam had invented a new way of tormenting Sadavir. He and several of his friends moved so as to be sitting behind Sadavir. They then started throwing small rocks, smuggled in for that express purpose, at the back of Sadavir's head when the teacher wasn't looking. Sadavir tried only once to appeal to the teacher.

"Excuse me, sir, the other boys just threw a rock at my head."

"Shut up, you little liar." The teacher snapped. "You should feel lucky just to be in the same class as normal children, don't go around spreading your Destroyer lies about them."

So the stoning continued. Sometimes the boys were inattentive and threw the rocks right under the teacher's nose. The teacher pretended not to notice and continued his droning about the many atrocities committed by the Destroyers. The teacher might as well have winked.

Soon the other boys wouldn't even pay attention to the lesson, but rather spend their time throwing rocks at Sadavir's head. Sadavir, after a few initial outburst that only brought ridicule and laughter from the other students, did his very best to ignore the boys and act as if he didn't feel the pebbles hitting him. I saw fire flash in his eyes, however, when the teacher made him clean up the rocks before he left class.

"If you must live like an animal, at least clean up after yourself."

Sadavir said nothing. I could see his hands trembling as he picked up the small rocks and carried them outside on his way home.

Everything came to an end, however, just a little while before his year mark in school. Having solicited no reaction from Sadavir, the other boys took to sneaking in larger and larger rocks. I grew concerned for Sadavir's safety as I saw the size of some of the stones that they were pelting against the back of Sadavir's head.

Padam pulled a rather large stone out of his pocket, and with a look of intense hatred, threw it hard toward Sadavir's head. He missed and the stone glanced off his neck, but the sudden pain made Sadavir yelp. The teacher turned on him.

"Didn't I tell you to be quiet during my lessons, whelp? One more outbreak like that and I'll take my stick to you."

Sadavir nodded. I saw Padam reach into his other pocket and pull out a similar stone. His arm reached far back behind him and threw the stone hard.

Without even thinking about it, I had already taken a step forward from my post at the wall. My role could only be as an observer, but a rock of that size could really hurt the boy or even kill him if it hit in just the right spot. My concern was unwarranted, however, and I watched, fascinated, as Sadavir's right hand snapped behind his own head, catching the stone just before it hit him. In the same fluid motion, he spun back to his left, whipping the stone around himself into a sidearm throw that sent the rock hurtling back at Padam.

The teacher had barely raised his eyes from his book, his attention drawn by the sudden movement, before the rock had slammed into Padam's nose and blood started streaming down his face as he erupted into loud wailing. I coughed into my hand to hide the smile that had crept involuntarily onto my face.

The whole class exploded into chaos as most of the children burst running from the dwelling, everything else forgotten. They had sat for hours on end hearing about the destruction and savagery of the Destroyers, they had no interest in witnessing it firsthand. The teacher fussed over Padam as his loud cries echoed through the small space, the whole village would be hearing about it soon.

Chapter 7

Cowards are always much more dangerous than heroes.
    –Musings of the Historian

I beckoned to Sadavir and we slipped discreetly out of the teacher's house and headed for home. I felt sincerely sorry for the boy. There would be no fairness in the story told. By the mere act of being born, he had been declared guilty of every crime imaginable.

Sadavir walked into the house, head bowed. Aric was just walking in through the back door, his face still sweating from the heat of his blacksmith's fire. One hand still held a hammer; the other was reaching for a dipper filled with cool water, placed there by Lauria, when he saw Sadavir.

"I'm sorry, Papa." Sadavir managed to get out before running to his room. Aric's eyes flashed to me and I offered a brief explanation. Aric's gaze lifted to the far wall, the one facing the village, as if he could see through the wall to the gathering mob. He shook his head.

"Make sure Lauria and Sadavir stay inside, won't you?" Aric asked. I nodded and he walked out the front door, his hammer still gripped in his hand. I gave Lauria strict orders to stay inside and to keep Sadavir from looking outside and then I slipped out the back door and around the house to watch the coming turmoil. Indeed, it didn't take long for the storm to crash on the house. I had barely made it around the house before a mob could be seen walking out to the house from the village. Saddhan was in the lead. He didn't even wait until he had reached the house before he started yelling accusations

"Your animal of a son attacked the children of the village! My own son was nearly killed! He's a menace to our village and he has to be taken care of."

The rest of the mob followed in his footsteps and gathered around him as he came to stand in front of Aric.

"Do you dare deny any of this, Aric?" Saddhan challenged. Aric didn't answer; he only stood like a wall between the mob and his home and family.

"Aric, you can't protect this freak forever, get out of our way, Aric, we won't be intimidated by you." Saddhan insisted. Aric still said nothing, only stood, hammer in hand, in front of Saddhan, glancing calmly over the crowd.

The effect was perfect. The crowd had expected yelling, fighting, for Aric to show that he was desperate and afraid. They needed him to show them that he was their enemy and that he was cornered and helpless. His silence and ready stance exuded confidence and readiness. Saddhan had suddenly fallen quiet, increasingly aware that he was within striking distance of Aric's hammer. He continued yelling as he edged his way back into the crowd.

"I tell you, Aric, we won't stand for this! Come on, let's get him!" Saddhan screamed. Aric still didn't move as the crowd started to move in on him. He knew the crowd all too well. They could become a mob and become brave, but when it came right down to it, there still had to be a first, the first person to step forward and start things going. Aric had a great advantage in the cowardice of Saddhan, had they had a leader who would step forward and take the first swing, then the mob would have followed and Aric would have been swarmed over and torn apart. As it was, Saddhan took no risks and had already taken the soul out of the mob by starting the retreat before the advance had even started.

As I watched would-be heroes step up, almost to Aric, then retreat; I was reminded of ocean waves breaking against a cliff. They could beat him together, they all knew it, but no one would be the first. The seconds dragged by and people started to feel more and more awkward. Aric finally broke his silence.

"Since my son is no longer welcome in your school, he will no longer go."

The mob fired again, glad for the concession and the chance to leave without looking cowardly.

"See that he doesn't! If we ever see him around our children again, Aric, you'll pay!"

With a few final shouted threats, the crowd dispersed and headed back to the village. I watched as Aric's shoulders dropped in a sigh of relief. He had been lucky, and he knew it. One brave man in that crowd would have meant disaster. He turned to head back into the house to inform Sadavir that he would no longer be attending school, an announcement that Sadavir accepted as a matter of course.

So Sadavir's education fell entirely into the hands of his father and mother. Realizing that it was only a little while before something else sparked the villagers' anger, Aric turned even more attention to Sadavir's training.

The next part of Aric's plan was a large contraption of metal bars. It was presented to Sadavir as a toy for his ninth birthday, even though the mess of bars stood four times his own height. His father explained that it was for climbing, so that Sadavir could see all around him. The boy smiled widely and ran to the bars, scrambling up as high as he could go with his rock tucked under one arm. It turned out to not be very far, since he very soon required two hands to go any higher, and one hand still held his constant companion.

He tried to swing from one side to the other just using one hand, but succeeded in only going about halfway, then falling. Both his father and mother moved to help, but the boy raised himself off the ground, stared at the bars, and started climbing again. This was to be a pattern that was repeated many times over.

Having been exiled from the village and completely ostracized by the other children his age, Sadavir's friends were his rock and his cage. By the time he was ten, he had succeeded in climbing to the very top of his twisted cage, tucking his rock, which had grown considerably in size by now, between his legs and using his arms to swing and pull himself up. He didn't have the impressive bulk of his father, but the sheer power contained in his lean sinews would have been impressive for a boy five years older than him.

Aric would occasionally head out to the cage with new bars and metal fittings, fresh from the forge. As the boy grew, so did the mess of bars, higher and more twisted. It became an impressive sight indeed. I was impressed with Aric's own dexterity as the large man would haul a bag of bars and fittings to the top of the cage to add to the vertical maze of metal.

Someone who didn't know Aric would have thought him

fearless, perched high above the ground, humming softly to himself. A closer look by those close to him showed gritted teeth and a paleness never before seen on the smith's ruddy face. The truth was he was scared to death, but he was dedicated to his son's training.

The cage itself became quite a sight to see. Every once in a while I would notice a curious villager watching from afar as Sadavir would weave and jump through the bars, like a spider skittering over its web. Always present was Sadavir's rock, whether tucked between his legs or under an arm. I was most impressed one day as Sadavir stood near the top of the cage, looking at a bar that was several feet away from him. Suddenly, he threw his rock high into the air and sprung, catlike, from the bar he was on to other one. Surprisingly, he didn't catch the bar with his hands, but rather overshot the bar by a few extra feet and caught the bar with his legs, hooking them at his knees. As he swung backwards, he caught his stone firmly in his hands.

I applauded in admiration. Sadavir, hanging upside down, his stone in his hands and his shirt hanging down around his arms, smiled sheepishly. I'm sure he would have blushed if his blood hadn't already rushed to his head from the stunt.

"Uncle Amar! Don't watch me!" He yelled, but he still looked pleased that someone had seen. I saw many other such stunts develop as time went on. Sadavir was just as happy jumping around his cage as he was on solid ground.

Although the boy still hadn't learned of his true purpose and hadn't spent even a single day fighting, his balance was superb, and his arms were strong and amazingly quick. It wasn't long before Aric had another task for his son.

"Sadavir, I need you to help your mother with the firewood. We are expecting a very cold winter, and these sticks are too big to fit in the fireplace, so I need you to break them, like this."

So saying, Aric placed one of the small sticks across two blocks and swiped his hand through the small stick easily, breaking it in half. And so it was that the blacksmith's son started breaking sticks with his hands while half a dozen axes leaned up against the tool shed.

The boy took to the task with the same resolve that he carried his rock or climbed his twisted cage. Just like the rocks, the twigs that he broke day by day slowly grew in size and strength. I noticed one day that he often hit the sticks in different places than the middle.

"Sadavir?"

"Yes, Uncle Amar?"

"Why do you hit the stick where you do?"

"That is where it is weakest."

"How do you know that?"

The boy just shrugged his shoulders.

"I don't know, I just do."

"Show me."

The boy proudly placed a large stick between the two blocks and stepped back, raising his hand, then passing his hand through the stick almost faster than my eye could follow. It wasn't only the quickness of his hand that caught my eye, however, it was his Stone. I thought I saw a ripple across the surface, just as I thought I had when he had caught the rock behind him at the school.

"Nicely done, Sadavir, you are becoming very strong."

The boy smiled, proud, but still a little embarrassed.

"Oh, it actually doesn't even hurt anymore as long as I break it, see?" And he held up his hand, displaying the toughened calluses that had formed on his hand. "My other one is tough too, see?"

He shifted his rock to his right hand and displayed the left, which was equally callused.

"Papa said that both hands should be tough, and that they should take turns carrying the rock."

"Oh, and he's certainly right, Sadavir."

Aric was always thinking up new "games" for the boy to do with his rock and his cage, combining speed and strength and forcing him to try new things to make it through his various challenges. It was obvious, however, that the boy didn't completely believe that all of these challenges were games. He set to every task with a determination and soberness that is rarely ever seen in boys of his age.

On his twelfth birthday, his father sat him down.

"Sadavir, do you know why I am needed in this village?" Aric asked.

"Yes, papa, you make all the metal things for everybody. Without you, nobody would have nails, nobody would have tools, nobody would be able to do anything." The boy's pride in his father was evident.

"Do you know what my Stone is for?"

"Yes, it helps you do your work, like Uncle Amar." I smiled at the comment. My usefulness in the family had been pegged as a cheap hand at the bellows.

"That's absolutely right, Sadavir. Now what are you going to do when you become a man?"

"I would like to be a blacksmith like you." Sadavir answered promptly.

"I would like that too, but you can't be." Aric's face had become somber.

"Why not?" Sadavir sensed his father's change in mood and asked the question quietly.

"Because you do not have a blue Stone like I do, you won't have that to help you do your work."

"Uncle Amar can still help me, that will be enough."

Aric smiled, "No, I'm afraid Uncle Amar won't be enough. Besides, you have your own Stone, which will help you do what you need to do to help the village."

"What do I need to do, papa?" The boy indeed had a very keen mind.

"Do you remember the stories we told you about the Destroyers?"

The boy's head fell, "The ones who killed Grandpa?"

"Yes, my son, those are the ones. Grandpa died because there was no one who was strong and brave enough to protect him."

"I'm strong and brave, papa, can I save people?" There was no trace of boasting in the boy's statement, just a simple knowledge of what he was capable of.

Aric smiled proudly, Lauria, watching on, had a small tear tracing down her cheek.

"Yes, son, that is what you will do, you will protect people against the Destroyers. But to do this, you will have to learn how to fight and defend yourself and others."

"Will you teach me, papa?"

"I will do what I can, Sadavir, but you will mostly have to learn by yourself. I will show you what the Destroyers will do, but you will have to decide what you will have to do to defend yourself."

The boy was silent for a moment, and then lifted his head.

"Papa?" Sadavir asked uncertainly.

"Yes, Sadavir?"

"The other people call me Destroyer... umm..." The boy trailed off, uncertain how to voice his question to his father. His father leaned down to grip Sadavir's shoulders and look into his eyes.

"You are a Creator, Sadavir, like me and your mother. Do you think those boys in school have ever met a real Destroyer?"

Sadavir shook his head.

"They don't even know what Destroyers are, so don't worry about what they say. Don't worry about them, when you start to save people, they will like you more, they will forget about the color of your Stone and they will get to know you and love you like we do."

Sadavir smiled gratefully.

"Ok, I think I can do that, can we start now?"

Aric nodded.

Chapter 8

I have never seen genius without a touch of madness... and vice versa.

–Musings of the Historian

"Stand in front of me." Aric commanded his son, sitting in a chair so that he would be on eye level with his son.

Sadavir obeyed.

"Ok, they will try to hit you, like this." Aric said, and then swung a ponderous fist at the boy, moving rather slowly to give the boy time to react. Sadavir didn't need the advantage. The fist hit empty air as Sadavir ducked under it.

"Why didn't you block it, Sadavir?" Aric asked.

"I didn't need to, papa." Sadavir stated simply. Aric thought for a moment, shrugged, and the training continued. Aric tried hits from different sides, slowly at first, giving Sadavir the chance to decide how he would handle it, then faster.

Every evening after dinner was cleared from the table, Sadavir would go and stand in front of his father. The attacks became quicker and more complex, working in combinations. Soon Aric had me attacking from the other side and Sadavir ducked, weaved and blocked through all of our attempts to find holes in his defenses. Lauria never fully accepted the training method. In the beginning, she would look on at her husband as he tried to hit their son with a pale, sick look on her face. Later, she gave up trying to watch and moved to a different room.

Aric also worked combinations into his other exercises. Now that Sadavir knew their true purposes, he worked with his cage and his rock religiously. Aric fitted stands into the cage so that sticks of wood could be set into them. Sadavir would fly through the cage, flipping around bars and spinning through tight spots, his hands flashing as he passed through, breaking the sticks as he passed.

Aric's ingenuity was tested almost daily through the next few years as he thought up new ways to prepare the growing Sadavir for the responsibility that he would be assuming later in his life. There was a grim nobility in his creativity. Always in the back of Aric's mind was the inevitable time when Sadavir would be fighting for his life. If he wasn't prepared, he would die. For Aric, that death would be directly on his own head. Every time he pushed his son harder, he was literally trying to save his life.

For his fourteenth birthday, his present was heavy iron bands that strapped onto his wrists and ankles. His rock, by that time, had grown too big to be practical and had been replaced by a ball of iron, just as heavy, but much smaller and harder to hold onto.

Sadavir's body seemed to rebel at every new attempt to chain him to the ground. If any of Aric's contraptions made him unable to leap through his cage like he regularly did, he would work long and hard, jumping and climbing, even just jumping up and down on the ground after it was too dark to see the bars of his cage. I think that Sadavir would have liked to have been born a bird, rather than a man.

It was inspiring to see him, with heavy iron bands around his legs and wrists, and with a heavy iron ball in tow, weaving through the iron bars of his cage with all of the agility of a squirrel.

Lauria openly worried about her son, always expecting him to fall from the metal monstrosity that now dominated the whole of her backyard and stood much higher than the house itself. Fortunately, she had stopped worrying about Aric always trying to hit Sadavir.

By the time Sadavir turned fifteen, we were already completely unable to hit him, even with both Aric and I attacking as fast as we could from both sides. He would sometimes block or deflect our blows, but much more often, our blows would land on empty air as Sadavir snaked away.

So, Aric took to trying to surprise the boy, striking out at him at unexpected times. Sadavir was never surprised, however, and Aric's massive fists would hit nothing. It was like fighting a wraith.

This only continued a short time as it proved even more ineffective than the usual system of attacks. There was nothing more two middle-aged men could do to prepare Sadavir for attacks from real warriors.

One day, Sadavir, Lauria, and I were eating breakfast. Aric was nowhere to be seen. Then suddenly the door opened and a very large wooden set of shelves moved its way into the room. It squeezed through the door and soon Aric could be seen on the other side, huffing and pushing. How he had carried the monstrous thing out to his house without help was beyond me.

"How do you like it?" He asked, beaming.

"Oh, Aric, it is very nice, and our old set of shelves did need replacing." Lauria said, eyeing the quality of the wood.

"Oh, yes, about that..." Aric hemmed sheepishly. "We're actually going to keep our old one too, Lauria."

"And why is that, Aric?" Lauria asked, her arms akimbo.

"Well, it still has plenty of years left in it, I would hate to throw away something that was still useful."

"Then why did you get this one?" Lauria demanded.

"Oh, well, I thought we could put Sadavir's stuff on it, his leg weights and things like that. They're very untidy, just stuffed in a box, wouldn't you agree?"

Lauria nodded slowly, eyeing her husband. She knew him too well to accept this at face value. To her credit, however, she didn't question him in front of Sadavir, but rather helped him as best she could as he maneuvered the heavy piece of furniture into the most awkward and illogical place in the middle of the room. Lauria started to object, but Aric put a finger to his lips and winked.

The next morning, a similar bit of furniture came in, unannounced, again, right after breakfast. This time, Lauria didn't even get up, only shook her head and stabbed viciously at her unfinished eggs. The bulk of wood took up another space of floor. I didn't understand what Aric was up to, unless it was his intent to crowd us right out of the house.

Lauria and I exchanged glances over breakfast the next day. Aric was gone again. Unsurprisingly, the door was knocked open again and the family was joined by one more giant piece of furniture. This time, he didn't even bother to offer an explanation.

Aric, with Sadavir's unquestioning help, rearranged the furniture in the house. When they finished, Aric looked pleased at the confused maze he had made of his house. That evening, we discovered the true purpose of the shelves.

Ambush.

Even Aric could hide behind the massive sets of shelves. Sadavir was no longer safe in his own home. At any time, Aric could jump out from behind one of those shelves. A few times he even had me clang his hammer on scrap metal out in the workshop so that Sadavir would think that he was working.

Sadavir had to learn how to get out of Aric's way in a hurry. Sadavir was quick and strong, but Aric was several times stronger still, his bear arms as hard as the metal they pounded. So, if Aric ever got a hold of Sadavir, it was a sure bet the boy would soon be tied up in Aric's tree trunk arms, his legs kicking in the air as he screamed and laughed.

I'll never forget the time when Aric tried to jump Sadavir right as he was going to bed, his iron bands and ball already put away. Aric was crouched just behind a shelf between the kitchen and Sadavir's room. When Sadavir passed, Aric leapt, panther style, at his son. Sadavir didn't even glance to the side to see his father. He just took to the air, leaping straight upward, tucking his legs under him. Aric's leap took him right under Sadavir and into the next shelf, sending it crashing into the far wall as Aric's bulk crashed into it. Sadavir landed lightly on his feet, staring at the scene of destruction before him.

The tension was broken as Aric started laughing from his position down on the floor. Sadavir laughed too and helped his father up off the floor.

It is not my role to give a complete description of everything that happens in these stories. My focus is the people that shape them. Still, I understand that someone reading this story might envision a home based in martial training and military discipline. Nothing could be farther from the truth. It was a home full of love and the warmth it brings. I hope one small reference may suffice to show what I mean.

I remember the day I went into the house to find Aric. I had reported for work and Aric wasn't there, the forge was cold. I warily entered the house to look for him. It wasn't all that uncommon for Aric to jump me, mistaking my footsteps for Sadavir's. I rounded one of the shelves to see Aric and Lauria wrapped in a warm embrace, swaying slightly to music only they heard. Aric saw me out of the corner of his eye and twitched his finger dismissively behind his wife's back. I took the hint and backed silently away to spend the day in my shed.

Some may find this instance quite irrelevant, but I can assure you, there is nothing that impacts a child so deeply as growing up in a home where the parents are in love with each other. I cannot help but wonder, in those moments, if I ever had parents, and if so, did they love each other?

Chapter 9

Fire can destroy or purify, strengthen or weaken, all depending on the nature of the material being burned. Pain has the same effects on the human soul, and for the same reasons.
–Musings of the Historian

A few days before Sadavir's sixteenth birthday, Aric sent him out with me to take a journey down the length of the wall to check for weaknesses or breaks. I was all too glad to be back on the road again. I was even gladder to get a chance to talk with the boy in private.

"I am glad you came with me, Sadavir." I began.

Sadavir smiled at me. "I'm glad I came too, Uncle."

"So how do you think your training is coming? Do you think you'll be ready to fight?"

Sadavir shrugged. "I'm not sure, Uncle, I've never been in a fight, I've never seen a Destroyer. Unless you count me." He added softly. I nodded.

"I'm surprised that there haven't been any more attacks since I've been here, although I'm glad you haven't had to fight before you were ready."

"Are the people glad that there haven't been any attacks, Uncle?" Sadavir truly didn't know much about the townspeople and what they felt or thought, they had seen to that.

"Some are, Sadavir, others blame me, others blame you."

"Blame?!" Sadavir started. "What is there to be blamed, isn't it a good thing that the Destroyers haven't come?"

"I'm afraid, Sadavir, that when things change without explanation, people tend to believe that something worse is coming. The people fear that the Destroyers are planning something much bigger, and that you and I are spies."

"Spies! How could I be a spy? I've never even seen a Destroyer, I've never known one, how could I be spying on them."

"Sadavir, there is something that you should have learned by now. People never allow reason to interfere with their fears. Have you ever wronged one of the townspeople?"

"Not that I know of, Uncle." He responded honestly.

"And yet, in spite of that, have they wronged you?"

Sadavir walked in silence for a moment. His hand crept up to the back of his head, remembering the sting of rocks.

"Yes, Uncle, they have. Why?"

"Because you are different."

"I know, but they are different from me, should I be hurting them for that?"

I smiled at the boy's simple logic.

"No, you should not be hurting them for that. That would do no good, and would only hurt you in the end."

"What do you mean, Uncle? They hurt me now and I haven't done anything to them. Maybe it's time they learned that they shouldn't do that." The boy's voice held a bitter edge.

"So you would like to hurt them back?" I asked.

Sadavir thought for a moment.

"Yes." He stated decisively. "They deserve it."

I nodded. "Of course they deserve it, but what would

happen once you hurt them back."

Sadavir paused to think. "More of them would come, like the day at school, and they would try to kill me, maybe my family too."

"So you see what I mean?"

"Yes, Uncle, but it's not fair!"

"I know, but life is not fair, Sadavir, and you must learn how to live as you know you must, in spite of injustice, that's what honor is."

"Honor?"

"Yes, Sadavir, honor. That is the only thing that separates you from them. If you started to hurt them back, you might win fights, but you will have become just like them, full of hate and fear. Is that what you want?"

Sadavir shook his head. "I will never be like them, Uncle, I promise."

I put my hand on his shoulder. "That's good to know, Sadavir."

We walked the rest of the evening in silence.

Very little else of consequence was said for the rest of the journey. After several days, our feet finally found themselves back on the streets of the village. Upon reaching Aric's house, Aric immediately rushed us to the back of the house, where he proudly displayed the true reason for why he had wanted Sadavir gone for a few days.

I was amazed at the ingenuity Aric had used in creating the contraption that I saw before me. At first, I couldn't even figure out what it was. There was a series of ramps with stone balls that ran down them, crisscrossing back and forth. A stone would start at the top of one ramp, run down to the end, and fall on to another ramp, heading a different direction. There were four series of ramps that ran together to form a sort of semi-circle around a white circle at the focus of the semicircle. At every level, there were strange contraptions attached to the ramps. They looked a lot like crossbows, although I had not seen anything so advanced among this people. The spring was supplied by a thin strip of steel that was bent back by a lever until it caught at a latch, then a small, perfectly round wooden ball was placed in the groove right by the latch. I looked for a triggering device and soon found out that the triggering device was set back on the ramps, so that they would be set off by the rolling stone balls. It looked like there was close to a hundred of the devices attached all over the massive network of ramps. All of them pointed toward the white circle in the center of the semi-circle. I began to understand.

Aric presented Sadavir with two steel armbands that clipped snugly onto his forearms.

Offering no other explanation than, "for blocking," Aric showed Sadavir into the middle of the circle. Stepping back, Aric started the stone balls down their tracks. As they reached the launchers, they would roll over the trigger that would launch the wooden balls, right at Sadavir.

The balls were only launched about as fast as a good toss, but as several launchers started to fire at once and from different angles, Sadavir found himself hard pressed to keep out of the way of the balls.

As the wooden balls shot toward him, he dodged from side to side, many of the balls missing him by very small margins. Although I had watched him train for more than ten years already, I was still amazed at his dexterity. He was able to contort his body, twisting and dipping away from the balls, it almost looked like some wild dance. Even so, it wasn't long until he was watching one ball too closely and was hit from behind by another. Distracted by the pain, he was hit by two others in a matter of seconds. Dazed, he lurched out of the circle and away from the launching balls. He looked apologetically at his father, but Aric only nodded.

The blacksmith had come up with another suitable challenge.

Chapter 10

A man only sees his destiny as he stands at the precipice of the unknown, and he only achieves it with the courage, at that moment, to step forward.

–Musings of the Historian

Sadavir took to the new challenge with the same intensity that he had met all the others. Every day, in spite of his mother's worried looks, he would walk out to behind the house where the fearsome semicircle patiently waited for him. He would turn the levers on all of the launchers until they were all loaded, and then stand in the circle while either Aric or I started the stone balls rolling down their ramps. Each time, he would dodge faster, or knock the balls out of the air before they could touch him, but each time, one would eventually find a way through his defenses and his mother would find one more bruise to frown at.

Aric, for his part, made sure that the challenge kept up with Sadavir. At night, he would change the launchers so that they would aim at different heights and launch at different times. That way, Sadavir could never get used to any particular rhythm or pattern.

An entire year passed before Sadavir could successfully stand in the circle and dodge or deflect all of the balls launched at him until all of the stone balls rolled out the bottom of their ramps and came to a stop on the soft ground. His mother clapped with joy. His father, with a mischievous look on his face, pulled a pack of metal strips from a sack and moved around to all the launchers, placing an extra strip next to the one already placed there. Having reloaded all of the launchers and pulling all of the levers to set them, we again set the balls rolling. Sadavir stood ready. The first one out of the launchers took Sadavir by surprise, as it shot out at twice the speed he was used to. He still managed to dodge or block about seven, but again one slipped through and again Sadavir was knocked out of the circle, gasping for breath after being hit much harder than ever before. The look Lauria gave to Aric was so fierce and Aric's expression so sheepish that I couldn't help but laugh.

Sadavir was well into his nineteenth year before he could stand successfully against all of the launched wooden balls. Once again, Aric pulled a new bag of strips from his side and added a third strip to the launchers. This time was more somber, however. With just two, Sadavir had already suffered a broken toe, a couple of broken fingers, and had even spent a few weeks bed-ridden with some broken ribs. I worried that if the new strips were like the last, then any ball that made it through Sadavir's blocks might seriously injure him, or even kill him. Sadavir seemed to sense the same thing and stood firmly in his circle, his fists clenched tight, the lean cords of muscle in his arms standing out like steel cables.

Something was different. I couldn't believe Aric would endanger his son's life so casually. I had no idea what Aric was thinking, but from the look on his face, he wasn't quite sure himself. Still, his determination was complete.

Lauria looked desperately at Aric, then at me, silently asking us not to go through with it. Not finding any give in Aric, and only quiet observation on my part, she turned and fled into the house, determined not to be a witness to what was about to happen. Although I shared her worry, I would not interfere. Aric remained stoic, but the heaving of his chest and the muffled sound of heavy breathing betrayed his anxiety.

With very strong tugs on the levers to load all of the launchers, it was a tense moment as we set the stone balls rolling down their ramps. I stood back to witness whatever might come. Aric's gaze was intense as he watched his son. He seemed to be waiting for something, expecting it.

Sadavir's face was like the steel he wore on his arms, determination etched deep into his face. The thing that caught and held my eye, however, was his Stone. It had been a permanent fixture for his whole life, so it had faded from conscious observation. I had stopped noticing it entirely.

I noticed it now.

I had seen it ripple faintly before, but now it shimmered and danced with a strange, dark light. It was as if all the darkest nights I had ever known had been trapped within that Stone and they now fought to break free. I believe this is what Aric had been waiting for.

I flinched as the first ball shot out at Sadavir. For a moment time stood still as my mind registered how fast the ball had left the launcher, it would certainly be fatal, Aric had gone too far, made a horrible mistake, I thought in that instant where only thought exists, independent of time.

Sadavir's arm blurred and the ball burst into pieces as Sadavir's steel armband crashed into it. What I then witnessed I will never forget, and the skill displayed I have never seen matched. Each ball, or even several balls would fire at him and each time they would be destroyed midair. Sadavir's eyes fixed a steady gaze forward, not even looking side to side at the incoming projectiles. He seemed to almost be in a trance similar to what I had seen in Aric when his Stone was alight.

His arms blurred in front of him and to both sides as if driven by their own life force. His body would twist one way or another with blinding speed. The Stone hanging around his chest blazed as if lit by a black fire. Time seemed to hang, meaningless. Cracking and snapping sounds twitched the air like the breaking of bones as Sadavir became an impenetrable force. Sound itself seemed to be out of sync. At last the stone balls finished their courses and the launchers fell silent. Sadavir stood in the faded white circle, his gaze still fixed forward, arms quivering at his sides. Around him was a widespread pile of destruction. Whether in halves or reduced to splinters, not a single wooden ball had survived the ordeal.

I looked over at Aric. He nodded slowly, but his mind seemed to be a million miles away, he looked on his son with an unreadable gaze. What he felt at that moment, I will never be able to say, what mixture of pride, awe, and maybe even a little fear.

The black Stone slowly dimmed and Sadavir slowly revived from his trance-like state. He looked toward his father.

"Papa, my arms hurt." Was all he said.

The armbands had bent onto his forearms. One of them we were able to unclasp, the other Aric had to carefully remove with his blacksmith tools. When we reentered the house, Lauria ran to her son and caught him in an embrace that lasted several minutes. Sadavir did not object or squirm, he only returned the embrace. Dinner was eaten in silence. Finally, Aric pushed his chair back and stood up.

"Sadavir, come here."

Sadavir quickly obeyed.

"Umm," Aric seemed unsure of how to proceed. "I have taught you everything I can. You are now ready to take your place as a defender of this people. Are you ready to take on this responsibility?"

Sadavir was silent.

"Son, are you having second thoughts?" Aric gently asked.

"Papa, I'm afraid." Sadavir answered.

Aric's eyes held great depths of emotion, his voice cracked as he answered.

"Son, after what I have seen you do, I don't think any Destroyers could hurt you. I'll make you new armbands, stronger ones. But you still don't have to do this if you don't want to."

Sadavir shook his head. "Papa, you didn't understand. I am not afraid of the Destroyers." He paused a moment before continuing.

"I am afraid of myself."

Aric looked to his wife, then back to his son.

"Why do you say that, son?"

"I can kill, papa. I never have, but I know that I can. How will I not lose my soul? How will I keep my honor?"

Aric looked as if someone had hit him in the stomach with one of his own hammers. He had obsessed about every part of his boy's training ever since the day Sadavir had been born, but this question he had never expected nor prepared for. Aric looked around desperately, but found no help. Lauria had begun crying softly.

It is my part only to observe, never to play any active part in

76

the stories that I tell, but sitting at that table and hearing the deafening silence that followed that question, I heard myself answering the question.

"I too have the power to kill, Sadavir." I began. "I could easily wait for someone to pass under a roof and I could drop a large stone onto their head. I could also hold someone under water until they were dead. All men have that power, to take life from others. This is a very great power.

"The thing you need to understand is that great power needs to be coupled with great responsibility. There are only two reasons to kill, Sadavir: to save your own life, or to save the lives of others. All other reasons change and shift with time, just as the mountains rise and fall.

"You have the power to kill, yes, you could even do it very easily. But you have another power, the power of choice. You have the skill to ensure that you will only kill when necessary, no one can make you kill against your will, that choice belongs only to you. And you will know when it is time. You will keep your honor."

Sadavir looked satisfied and turned back to his father, resolved.

"Papa, I am ready to become a protector of this people."

Aric smiled proudly and put his hand on Sadavir's shoulder. The look he shot me spoke of endless gratitude for answering the question he could not.

"When I finally became a true blacksmith after being an apprentice for many years, there was a ceremony where I was presented with a new hammer that had never been used to begin my new life as a blacksmith. I can't think of a ceremony that we could have for you; your tools are your hands, your feet, and your wits. So, I suggest that I just shake your hand and you hug your mother. Be sure to take your handkerchief."

Sadavir smiled and took his father's outstretched hand, gripping it firmly. He then walked over to his mother and gave her a hug as she smiled and sniffled through her tears of many emotions.

Chapter 11

Music makes absolutely no sense at all. Perhaps that is the point.
–Musings of the Historian

The night became one of celebration. Aric danced Lauria around the floor as Sadavir and I laughed and drummed and clapped our hands, supplying the music. Lauria finally collapsed into a chair, breathing heavily.

"Say, the night is still young, I'm betting that Paritosh still isn't quite done closing up his baker's shop, perhaps he still has some of his sweet breads for sale. Amar, why don't you and Sadavir run down there and see if he'll open up for you, he owes me for the new hinges on his door anyway." Aric suggested.

Sadavir happily followed me out of the door and into the cool evening air. The sun was just barely starting to disappear below the horizon and the dim light created an odd look to the village, as if it were all just one big painting on a master's canvas.

The baker, although not exactly happy about it, stopped sweeping his floor long enough to open the door for us and give us some sweet breads. Although not truly requiring anything to eat, I had become quite fond of the breads of this village; their quality matched the superior workmanship of everything else.

Music came from the town square and the sounds of loud laughter floated across the cool air to our ears. On most nights, the sound would have caused Sadavir to drop into a melancholy as he caught the merest taste of a world he wasn't allowed to enter. Tonight however, the joy of others couldn't match his own. He had pleased his parents and had finally gained a sense of who he was in the world. Few men indeed can claim the same at any age.

Skirting the city square, we walked in the shadows on the outer rim of the village. My nose suddenly caught a slight smell on the air, easily recognizable as cheap wine of local vintage.

"Hey look, it's the freaks!" A drunken voice shouted out, all too familiar, answered by laughter. Sadavir looked irritated, but we walked on.

"Hey, don't leave now, we're having a great party, maybe you could come have fun with us." The voice shouted out. Again, there was no response from Sadavir or myself. I heard the sounds of running feet coming up on us from behind. Sadavir also heard them and turned to face them. There were about six of them, all just a little older than Sadavir and it was quite obvious that they had been drinking.

"So, outsider," Started the leader, who had been yelling at us earlier. In the dim light I could still see that it was Padam. "What are the women like from your land? They must be very ugly if you left entirely."

The others laughed and Padam, encouraged, continued.

"Or maybe there's nothing wrong with your women, maybe you were just too ugly and stupid to get one to marry you. I'm glad to see that you're choosing good friends, Sadavir."

"Leave us alone, Padam, we weren't bothering you." Sadavir retorted.

Padam laughed, and then put on an act of looking hurt,

80

"Oh, you find us bothersome? That's hurtful, Sadavir, I thought we were friends."

Then the act dropped and Padam's voice dripped with the same venom I had heard from his father on several occasions.

"Now you listen to me, you freak. You are the one who is a bother, you and your outsider friend. Every second the two of you are here the village isn't safe. You aren't like us, you're like mud in the drinking water and you don't belong here. I know your daddy would get so upset if anything ever happened to you, so we won't hurt you this time."

The mood was getting ugly. Although part of it myself, I couldn't help but observe the situation unfold with an almost morbid fascination.

"But your 'uncle' has never been welcome here, and maybe it's time he moved on." Padam snapped his fingers and several of the boys rushed forward, grabbing my arms and holding me still. I didn't resist. The other three pulled knives from their belts and stood around Sadavir, ensuring that he wouldn't try to interfere. Padam then turned his attention to me.

"So, they call you Amar, don't they? Fine name, but I think you stole it."

Padam slid a knife from his belt and walked slowly toward me.

"You have known for almost twenty years now that you are not welcome here. Why do you still stay? I don't know what kind of plan you have for this village, or what kind of…" Padam smiled as he searched for his next words, "…'benefits' you are receiving living over there under Aric's roof."

Padam paused to smile smugly at Sadavir.

"But there are plenty in the village who want to see you gone, and I think now is a good time."

Padam stopped talking and moved toward me with his knife, this time with purpose. I felt the two young men who were holding my arms tighten their grips. The smell of wine lay heavy on the still night air. The knife started to move towards my stomach and suddenly there was a slight sound of a scuffle to the side, where Sadavir was. Padam's head whipped around to see what had happened. In the failing light, he couldn't see much. What was certain was that two of the men were already writhing on the ground. Only one remained standing and he had both hands clenched around his thigh as a dark stain started to spread down the leg of his pants.

That flash of a glance was all that Padam had before Sadavir was on top of him. Padam swung his knife hard at Sadavir as he closed on him. Sadavir's hand flashed and with the sound of a muffled snap, the knife fell to the ground and Padam pulled his broken arm protectively into his stomach, wailing loudly. Even the darkness of the night could not hide the dark light dancing across the surface of Sadavir's Stone.

The two men holding my arms abandoned their posts and ran for the safety of the village square, yelling for help.

"Are you ok?" Sadavir asked, his voice was calm.

"I'm fine, thank you." I replied, "But we had better get home, nothing good will come of this."

"I didn't want to hurt them." Sadavir said as we started walking toward his home.

"I know you didn't"

"They were going to hurt you, maybe even kill you."

"Maybe."

Sadavir walked in silence for a few more paces, then something else occurred to him.

"Uncle, you didn't seem afraid of him, did you not see the knife?"

"I saw it."

"Then why didn't you fight?"

"That is not my path."

"What would you have done if I hadn't fought them?"

"I would have wandered on."

"But Uncle, what if he had killed you?"

I merely smiled sadly in the darkness and left his question unanswered.

Aric was standing outside the door as we came home, looking towards the commotion in the town.

"What happened?" He asked anxiously.

"Some men from the village attacked us, they were going to hurt Amar." Sadavir answered.

Aric nodded, he did not ask how things went after that.

"You had better get inside."

Sadavir meekly obeyed and I exchanged glances with Aric as I walked inside. He knew as well as I the consequences of what had been done. A very tender balance had existed in the village for years now. Hatred and intolerance festered like a wound, fed constantly by Saddhan and his men filling the people's ears with stories of what Sadavir would one day do to them if they continued to let him live. They had also had a long time to consider their own cowardice, such things weigh heavy on a man's soul. Something like this would break the floodgates wide open. Inside, Sadavir sat, head in hands as Lauria hovered over him protectively. Already, shouts could be heard in the distance.

It was only a matter of time before footsteps were heard outside and Saddhan's distinctive voice was heard to call out.

"Send him out, Aric, you can't protect him this time."

Aric's head bowed for just a moment, then he rose and strode to the door, stepping out into the night air. Sadavir and I followed after, taking up positions to either side of Aric.

"He's a monster, Aric, there's no denying it now. It's only luck that he didn't kill my son or the others." The lights from the torches that the villagers carried danced in Saddhan's eyes, the man almost looked pleased that things had come to this.

"He was attacked, Saddhan, he was only defending himself and Amar." Aric's deep voice was calm and firm.

"Oh, of course! As if he would actually tell you if he had attacked them, how else could have badly injured them before they could even fight back? I have the word of six of our finest young men attesting to the fact that they were merely laughing and having a good time when Sadavir attacked them."

Aric's voice hardened. "Are you calling my son a liar, Saddhan?"

"Now, now, Aric, let's not make this a personal affair. I am merely a spokesperson for the village, and they will not be bullied by you again."

Glancing out over the crowd, I could see that he was right. The fear and suspicion that they had been harboring for more than twenty years had finally reached the point where it outweighed the risk of possible harm from Aric. The events of the evening were only a spark in a dry forest. Aric could sense it too, but he was not about to hand over his only son to the mongrel horde that stood at his door. He reached just inside the door and picked up his hammer off of the chair, where he had placed it earlier.

"Very well, Saddhan. If you must have my son's blood to appease your bitterness, so be it, but I promise you that your blood will flow with it. Come as you please." Aric finished and settle into a wide stance, hammer at the ready. The villagers, packed tightly together, as no one wanted to be the first to reach the man, still moved forward, intent on removing Aric from the steps.

"Wait!"

Surprisingly, the cry came from Sadavir. He moved out from behind his father to stand in front of him.

"I will go over to live with the Destroyers." The announcement had a mixed effect on the crowd, some grasped at the chance for compromise, while others seemed even more desperate to keep Sadavir from joining their enemies.

"We can't trust you, boy." Saddhan sneered. "And even if we could trust you to leave, what promise do we have that you won't come over the wall again someday to kill us and steal from us."

Sadavir's eyes were cold. "I am offering you no promise at all, no concession, Saddhan. I am offering these people a chance to live through the night, because I still consider myself a protector of this village until I am out of it."

Saddhan laughed out loud. "Do you honestly think that your father can fight us all, boy?"

Like a snake striking, Sadavir shot across the small space of ground and had Saddhan by the throat before the man even knew what was happening. Saddhan choked as he pulled and battered against Sadavir's arm, but to no avail.

Aric, the master blacksmith, had sculpted a piece of steel out of his son.

Several from the mob tried to save their leader. Sadavir silently and effectively repulsed their efforts, cracking hands that tried to grab his arms, snatching the thrown torches out of the air and throwing them back at their owners, all without loosening his grip on Saddhan's neck. Finally, he let go and Saddhan slumped to the ground, wheezing and coughing while he groped in the dust.

Sadavir looked up at the rest of the mob.

"I was to be your protector, do not make me your destroyer. If it is the wish of the village that I leave, I will leave in the morning. You may try to kill me or drive me out before then, but you see the last of my mercy in the writhing worm at my feet."

So saying, Sadavir turned to walk back inside, whipping around only once to catch a rock that had been thrown at the back of his head. That was the last straw; the crowd broke and ran in all directions, tripping over each other like sheep fleeing from a lion. Sadavir watched them for a moment, let the rock fall to the ground, then turned and walked back inside. As he reentered the house, the iron drained out of him and he fell into his mother's arms, weeping. Aric simply hung his head and walked out the back door. I stood watching the scene in front of me.

After a short while, Lauria left Sadavir where he sat to go and prepare as much provisions as she could for his upcoming journey. Sadavir, as if sensing the energy he would need for the road ahead, laid down and quickly fell asleep.

I heard the roar of the bellows and the clang of hammer on metal coming from Aric's shop and I crept silently out to peek through the small ventilation window. Aric stood illuminated by the red light of the fire, with a small island of blue light shining on his chest. He pounded on a red-hot piece of metal as if it were the cause of all the injustices he had suffered for the last twenty years. Tears flowed freely down his face and fell onto the piece of metal he was working on, sputtering and skipping on the hot metal until they were smashed into steam under the next blow of the hammer.

Chapter 12

Every once in a while, nature gives an ear to the moods of men.
Heat for their envy, thunder for their rage; but most of all, rain
for their sorrow.

-Musings of the Historian

The next morning, the rain fell in a grey drizzle. In spite of
the weather, the mob was back at their door in the morning to
escort Sadavir to the wall. This time, I noticed, almost all of them
were carrying weapons of some sort, some carried farm
implements or clubs, but most carried rocks. I smiled as I viewed
them through the open door.

Aric entered the room where Lauria and Sadavir waited. He
presented Sadavir with new armbands, stronger ones than before.
Sadavir took them gratefully. He looked at them carefully. I could
see small symbols carved on the armbands, a different one on
each of them.

"I won't forget, Papa." He said. Aric just nodded, his Adam's
apple working up and down as he fought back the emotions
welling up inside of him.

Lauria handed a pack to Sadavir and hugged him again.
Aric pulled me to the side and spoke in hushed tones.

"Amar, you know that you are like a brother to us, and you
are always welcome here. I was just wondering…" He paused, not
knowing how to finish.

I smiled and raised my hand.

"I will go with Sadavir, but I expect that it will be him who will look after me." Aric nodded gratefully. "Besides, this story is not yet done, but it will continue on the far side of the wall with Sadavir, I made up my mind to follow him long before now."

Aric looked as if he still didn't understand what I was saying, but his gratitude was visible in his bloodshot eyes. At that moment, he looked very old.

Lauria had also fixed a pack for me and I hoisted it onto my shoulders and took my place next to Sadavir.

Aric walked over to stand next to Sadavir. He took a moment and helped his son snap the new armbands into place. They fit his arms perfectly, another tribute to the care and skill that Aric had poured into them during the night.

"I think it best if we say our goodbyes here, son, I don't want the image of you going to the far side of the wall in my mind." Aric admitted. Sadavir nodded.

No words were spoken, father and son simply embraced. The master blacksmith had crafted his finest work and now had to let it go.

At length, Sadavir turned from his father and walked through the mob, barely noting their existence. The mob, in turn, took great troubles to keep a fair distance from the youth. I followed in his wake. The mob followed me.

We headed out of the village and traveled north along the wall. As we passed the center of town, Saddhan leaned out the front of his shop, intent on one more try at the boy.

"You can't allow this!" He demanded. "He should be killed! We can't let him join the Destroyers!"

His yelling lasted until the last of the people had passed him by, then he yelled at their backs. But then, the tone had become more pleading.

"Make sure you put him through quickly, and lock the gate up tight, don't let the Destroyers in while you're locking him out. Be quick!"

Others had packed provisions, so I assumed that the trip would be a long one. I leaned in closer to Sadavir.

"Where is it that we're going?" I queried.

"There's a gate." He said. "Papa told me about it this morning."

"Why would they build a gate if they never planned on crossing over?" I wondered out loud.

"Papa said that no one really knows. It is the oldest part of the wall; no one really knows how long ago it was built. Papa said that he walked there once when he was younger. He said that the design is better at the north part. He said that the rest of the wall just looks like an imitation of the northern portion. The rest looks like it was copied from that."

"I guess we'll see." I remarked. Sadavir nodded, his head lowered. The mood was somber all around. For Sadavir, he had to leave his friends and family. For the others, they still feared him, but couldn't do anything about it. I was surprised to notice that Saddhan and most of his men weren't present with the rest of the company. I had thought that Saddhan would have been the first in line to watch as Sadavir left the village.

I couldn't put my finger on it just yet, but I had the feeling that Saddhan was hiding something. Whether it was something at the wall or something he was doing back at the village, I didn't know. When people start acting contrary to their own nature, it is a fairly good indicator that there is an unseen motive driving them.

Even surrounded by the surly crowd, it felt good to be traveling again. While I had enjoyed my stay with Aric and his family, it was one of the longest stretches I had ever spent in one place.

The country stayed the same, but over the wall, I could see that we were approaching mountains. A thought occurred to me.

"Sadavir?"

My voice broke him out of his sullen reverie.

"Hmm? What is it, Uncle?"

"What is to stop the Destroyers from walking around the wall?"

"At the north, the wall butts us against overhanging cliffs. No one has ever been able to climb those cliffs." Sadavir answered absentmindedly. "On the south it goes into the sea."

"Why don't they just swim around?" I queried further. Sadavir shrugged his shoulders. Surprisingly, it was one of the men from the mob who spoke up to answer my question.

"There are fish along the coast who will attack anything that enters the waters." The man who spoke was Baldev, a Creator with a red Stone who often argued with Saddhan about how things should be done. He was a good man who never really hated Sadavir like the others did, but lacked the courage to ever say anything about it.

There were a few like that in the village. They were more tolerant and reasonable than the rest of the villagers, but they lacked the backbone to ever do anything about their convictions.

91

Several of them were here now in the group. I suspected that they were partially there to help protect Sadavir. There were others in the group who would gladly have killed him the second they were out of sight of the village.

My suspicions were confirmed that night when we set up camp. Several of the men set up watch on Sadavir. Baldev set up men to watch the watchers. Through it all, Sadavir acted like a man in a trance. He had lost his family, the only other people he had ever really known. He had done nothing wrong but be born. He had never wanted anything from these people but acceptance. All that was gone now. A new and better life might be awaiting him, or it might not. He waited like a man in limbo, tortured by his past and haunted by his future. He lay close to me as the rest of the men settled in to sleep.

"Uncle, what do you think it will be like over there?" He whispered.

"I have no idea." I replied frankly.

"Do you think they'll try to kill me?"

"Yes."

He fell silent again, thinking.

"Do you think I'll see my parents again, Uncle?"

"If you truly want something, Sadavir, you will find a way to obtain it."

He rolled over to face me.

"But Uncle, my parents can't come over to the Destroyers' side, I couldn't protect them forever, I still don't know if I'll be able to protect you. And of course the people won't ever let me come back here, even if I could find a way over the wall."

"Do you think they could stop you, Sadavir? Think of what

happened last night."

He chewed that over for a minute and nodded. "I guess they couldn't, but I wouldn't be able to stay, they would always be trying to kill me."

"You're probably right, Sadavir. The only thing I can say is that things do change. Maybe you will find a way to be accepted among your own people again."

"Maybe." He said, and rolled back onto his back to fall asleep. It wasn't long before his breathing became slow and steady. In spite of his traumatic day, his sleep was undisturbed and peaceful all through the night.

The next day was spent in the same sort of tense silence until we reached the gate. The gate itself was a daunting thing. It was made of solid steel, crafted to the space so as not to leave even a finger-sized hole anywhere in its construction. Several men from the village went ahead of Sadavir to lift the enormous crossbar from its position and open the mighty doors. I wondered again at the craftsmanship of the people, for the door opened easily, with barely a creak from its ancient hinges. Wouldn't even the finest workmanship fade at some point, I wondered?

Sadavir walked through the doors, not pausing to look back or to speak to any of the villagers, he had left them a long time ago, or rather, they had left him. We walked through the gate and it closed behind us with a ground-jarring thud.

It felt good to have new ground under my feet.

Chapter 13

I can sum up everything I've learned about effective hand fighting thusly: Swiftly connect a hard surface of yours to a soft surface of his.

–Musings of the Historian

I followed Sadavir, who seemed to have no other intention but to walk aimlessly through the new country, head hung low. That didn't last very long however, as there seemed to be Destroyers who kept watch on the gate. Three men started shouting and pointing at us. Their shouts carried the same tone I had heard when I had first entered Surac; only the words were different.

"Creators! Creators!"

One man turned and ran into the brush, the other two advanced on Sadavir.

"Where are the others, boy? What sort of trickery is this?" The man who spoke wore a scar on his face and carried a crude spear at his side. Both men looked suspicious, but ready for anything. There was none of the intense fear that the Creators wore so well.

Sadavir didn't even raise his head, but continued walking.

"Hey boy! I believe I asked you a question!" The man stood directly in front of Sadavir and leveled his spear at his chest. Sadavir's left hand snapped up to grab the end of the spear. His right forearm slammed into the weapon not far from his hand, the steel armband snapping easily through the thin wooden pole. The man jumped back to his companion as Sadavir threw the useless spearhead on the ground.

His companion drew two long knives from his belt and charged Sadavir. Unlike the clumsy drunks back in the village, these men moved with cat-like agility, they were no strangers to violence. They focused on the boy, not giving much attention to me, though both of them still took great pains to avoid showing their backs to me.

The knives flashed in with blinding speed but only clanged on Sadavir's armbands. The man jumped back before Sadavir could counter-strike. His move had only been one of diversion so that his friend could circle around Sadavir to attack from the other side. The broken spear shaft spun in the other man's hands. It was a different weapon now, but he still knew it well. Now both circled around Sadavir. As if acting on some secret signal, they both attacked at once.

The man with the knives had to twist out of the way to avoid getting hit with his friend's staff as their attack clashed on empty air. Sadavir had dropped low to the ground, wiry and feral. The man with the spear hit the ground hard as his legs were swept out from under him by Sadavir's foot and the man with the knives was driven back under a fierce assault from Sadavir, who pounced from the ground like a panther. The knives clanged a few times on the armbands before they were knocked from the man's hands and the man tripped backwards. Sadavir's left hand whipped behind him to catch the shaft of the spear that had been thrust at his back. Pulling the spear towards him as he twisted, the man was jerked forward and tripped, falling onto his own friend as the spear was again jerked from his hand.

They both looked up at Sadavir with fear in their eyes, expecting Sadavir to finish them off now that they were both helpless. Sadavir instead flicked the spear onto the ground in front of them, turned, and resumed his slow, sulking walk. I followed, but watched over my shoulder as the two men got up and scrambled off into the trees.

So those were the Destroyers, I thought to myself, once the excitement of the battle was over. Their clothes were rough, mostly made of animal skins or very crude cloth. The difference between the cultures was a familiar one: the Creators were the farmers, the builders; the Destroyers were the hunters and gatherers, probably nomadic.

We wandered all that day. When we settled in for the night in a green meadow, I could hear rustling in the shadows. They had not yet decided what to think about this newcomer who could fight so well.

The morning found Sadavir in a more talkative mood.

"Amar, what do you think they'll do next?"

"Well, they will decide that they need to kill you as quickly as possible with the least amount of danger to themselves."

Sadavir nodded and turned his attention back to the cold bit of bread that represented the whole of his breakfast.

Later that day, as we walked through the forest, Sadavir was barraged with stones from the treetops. For a few seconds, the calm of the forest was shattered with the dull cracking sound of rocks bouncing off of steel. No sooner had the rocks hit the ground than Sadavir counterattacked, scrambling into the trees like a squirrel and driving the Destroyers to the ground as they fled from him. They started to run, but only to regroup. There were about ten of them this time. They approached Sadavir warily. I recognized one of them as the man who had wielded the spear the previous day. Most looked as if they had left their weapons in the trees, but those who had them pulled knives as they circled in around Sadavir. Those without knives rushed in, a decoy attack to draw Sadavir's attention. The ruse failed as Sadavir leapt over them, leapfrogging over the leader's head. As soon as he hit the ground, Sadavir threw his body backwards against the knees of his attackers. The attackers barely had time to spin around before their legs were swept out from under them.

The ones with knives had rushed in to help their fellows and several tripped over their friends as they hit the dirt. Sadavir did not waste the moment of confusion. He wove through the mass of men, hands flashing. Knives fell from bruised or broken hands and the men retreated, several holding their wounded limbs. They stood about ten feet from Sadavir, unsure what to do. These men were brave, and not likely to quit, but everything they had tried so far hadn't even succeeded in scratching Sadavir. The only mark of battle was the dirt on his body from the quick scramble after tripping them.

This was outside their concept of reality. The boy was obviously a Creator, but he did not cringe or beg for his life as they had first expected. More than that, he was just a boy who had only been shaving for a couple years. They didn't know what to think.

Sadavir moved to make up their minds for them. He reached down, picked up a rock, and without even standing up, launched it from the ground and hit one of the men in the head. The man slumped to the ground, unconscious. Those who still had full use of their hands grabbed their downed companion and they disappeared into the woods. We weren't bothered again for the rest of the day. That might by the fire, Sadavir surprised me with a question.

"Amar, who are you?"

"What do you mean?"

Sadavir shrugged, "I'm not quite sure, I've grown up knowing you only as my Uncle Amar, but that's not who you are, that is not even your true name. It didn't really matter before, but now you are the only person I know in the world, and I don't even know who you are. So who are you?"

I saw no need for deception at this point, so I answered him simply.

"I am the Historian."

Sadavir only looked more confused.

"What is a historian?"

"A historian is a storyteller."

Sadavir accepted my simplistic explanation and continued with his questioning.

"So why have you chosen to follow me?"

"Because this is an interesting story, Sadavir. I wish stories about happy people leading successful lives were more interesting, but they're really not."

"But I still don't understand why you're following me, why didn't you stay back at the village, or move on to some other village to see what stories they might have there? Why waste your life following a single story?"

"Because it is new, Sadavir. I could tell you exactly what is happening back at the village, that is a story that has been replayed hundreds of times. This story is new, I don't know what tomorrow will bring."

"You are indeed a strange man, Uncle."

I only smiled in response and Sadavir continued with his questions, glad to have something to distract his troubled thoughts.

"Where do you come from? I mean before you came to live with my father. And how is it that you chose to become a historian?"

"Tell me this, Sadavir, how is it that you chose to become a warrior?"

"I didn't choose, Uncle, this life chose me." Sadavir shrugged his shoulders. "I wanted to be a blacksmith."

"And I wanted to be a stone cutter."

Sadavir nodded and laid down. Before he drifted off to sleep, he raised his head.

"Uncle?"

"Yes, Sadavir?"

"You never answered my other question."

"Which one?"

"Where do you come from?"

"I guess I didn't."

Sadavir gave an exasperated sigh, turned over, and went to sleep.

Chapter 14

Few things disarm a man so quickly and completely as honest friendliness.

–Musings of the Historian

In the morning, a strange sight met our eyes. A man, unarmed, sat near the fire, stirring the coals and putting on more wood. Sadavir rose into a crouch, tensing like a snake before it strikes. The man only smiled.

"Take it easy there, son. I am not here to hurt you. I am only hoping that you will not hurt me. My name is Andre." The man said and offered his hand to Sadavir. Sadavir stared at the hand, then searched the trees around the clearing. He shifted the steel bands on his forearms for a snugger fit. The man smiled.

"Don't worry, I am alone. I only wanted to talk. My men inform me that a god is walking through our land, one that cannot be killed. I know that my men are not fools, although they are superstitious." The man's hand was still extended, although it seemed like both he and Sadavir had forgotten it entirely.

"So, I have come to tempt my fate, speaking to this young god who dresses like a Creator and trespasses in our land."

Sadavir was still tense, but he rose to his feet and took the man's hand.

"My name is Sadavir. I am no god, but merely an outcast from my own people. I did not choose to come to your land."

Sadavir's tone lowered.

"But make no mistake, I have nowhere else to go, so if anyone tries to force me to leave, I will fight."

Andre again smiled. "Yes, I caught that part. According to my men, you fight like the very Devil and sprout four more arms in battle. So far, I only count two." Andre winked.

"So why are you here, Andre. I don't believe for a second that you just came to get acquainted and then slip back into the brush." Sadavir wasn't amused by Andre's attempted jests.

"Well then, to tell you the truth, I was wondering if you might like to visit my village. Lovely place this time of year."

Andre smiled again, but again was only met by a blank stare from Sadavir. Andre explained further.

"Between all of their superstitious ranting, my men told me that you have a Destroyer's Stone, but one like they've never seen before. Now, how you came to be exiled to this land, I don't know, but if you are a Destroyer, then you belong with us."

"And I am to believe that you will simply welcome me with open arms into your village?" Sadavir was skeptical.

"Well," responded Andre. "The way I see it, there is a risk involved, but there will be a risk anyway. I haven't seen you forage anything from the land, which means that you are living entirely on what you have in those packs. If you can't live off the land, then that means you must get more food when those packs run out. That means stealing from us. And frankly, I would a lot rather offer you food with an open hand than lose that hand trying to defend my village from you."

Sadavir tried to keep his face expressionless, but I could see that he hadn't thought about that before. He had never had to survive outside of the protective walls of his own home. Andre's offer suddenly seemed very appeasing.

"How do I know that you will not simply try to kill me in my sleep?" Sadavir asked, still clinging to his suspicion of a trap. Andre chuckled again.

"Well, the first problem I would have with that is getting any of my men to follow my order. Your iron arms have robbed my men of their courage, they think you indestructible. The truth of the matter is that we would gain very little in having you dead, but if the attempt went wrong, I suspect we would pay a very heavy price for our treachery. As the leader of my village, that is not a chance I am willing to take, if you're even half as good as my men say you are. So, what do you say?"

Sadavir turned to me, the first time either one of them had taken note of me during the whole conversation.

"What do you think, Uncle?"

"You decide what you will, Sadavir, I will be right behind you." Sadavir turned back to Andre, accepting the fact that he would get nothing more out of me.

"Very well, I will go with you."

"Great, I'm sure you both could use a hot meal."

Sadavir's tough cool was slowly melting as his heart opened to the possibility of a new life, one of acceptance.

After we had packed up, Andre led off and the two of us followed. The walk was surprisingly short. We had walked less than a hundred yards through the dense brush when the shadow of a path suddenly opened to reveal a bustling village. The homes were rounded in shape and made out of animal hide stretched over wooden poles. Children laughed as they played with a heavy ball in the middle of the village, trying to push it past each other with large sticks. Andre laughed out loud at the expression on Sadavir's face.

"You see, I was going to wait a couple of days, maybe let your food run out a little more before I tried talking with you, but since you already stood at our door, I thought I might as well ask you in."

Andre led them to one of the huts, pulled back the flap and started to step in. He only made it halfway in before a woman's arms snaked around his neck and pulled him in.

"I'm glad you're back. Are you all right?" A decidedly feminine voice interrogated from inside the dwelling. "Is he truly a god?"

Andre laughed. "No, he is not a god, but he is young, he is hungry, and he is waiting outside our door."

The voice gasped and the flap was torn to one side and a rather pretty looking woman waved us in.

"Allow me to introduce my wife, Nadya." Andre said.

"Nice to meet the two of you. I'm so sorry I left you standing out there; I didn't know that he was going to bring you back so soon. Are you really Creators? You don't even have a Stone. Oh, he said you were hungry. Are you hungry? I'll get you both something to eat, just sit down and talk to Andre and I'll have something fixed in no time at all."

Before either of us could even introduce ourselves, she was gone again, retreating through a flap that separated the hut into halves. Andre smiled and motioned for us to sit down.

"Don't worry, there will be plenty of time to talk with her once your bellies have been filled. In fact, you will have a hard time avoiding it. In the meantime, I was wondering if I might have a look at your Stone, The rumors I heard from my men have gotten me curious."

Sadavir was still wary, but he was disarmed by his friendly surroundings and removed the Stone from around his neck, handing it to Andre. Andre, in turn, fished around in a small pouch he wore at his side and handed his own Stone to Sadavir. It was blue, much like Aric's except for the fact that this one was opaque, like Sadavir's. Andre studied Sadavir's Stone carefully, as if trying to draw some secret from it. Finally he shrugged his shoulders and handed it back to Sadavir. He then turned his attention to me.

"And you, I am so sorry for having ignored you all this time, what was your name?"

"Oh, I have been known by a great many names, why don't you just pick one for me, something that will be easy for you to remember."

Andre smiled, then turning his head, he yelled to his wife. "Honey, it appears that we have a new son, what shall we name him?"

I was struck by the similarities between Andre and Aric. I think that in different circumstances, the two would have been very good friends.

His wife stuck her head out of the flap. "What are you talking about, husband?"

"Well, it seems that these travelers have come to us quite unprepared, this one seems to have even forgotten to bring a name along with him. Do we have one we can lend him?"

Nadya shook her head and rolled her eyes at the grinning

Andre, not answering, and pulled her head back through the flap.

"Oh well, it looks like I'm on my own. I think I shall call you Sergei. You look like a Sergei."

"Sergei it is then." I replied.

"So, Sergei, do you also hide an interesting Stone somewhere?"

"I actually have no Stone. I am not of this people."

"My, my, there is no end to the surprises this morning. Where are you from then?"

"I come from a land beyond the horizon."

"That must be nice, I tried to go there myself once, but the horizon kept moving out of my reach each day."

I smiled. "It happened much the same way with me."

At that moment, Nadya came bustling back through the flap, pottery bowls in both hands and another perched precariously on her head. She laid the steaming bowls in front of us and retrieved the bowl from on top of her head and also set that in front of us. Having done so, she sat down next to her husband and looked at us expectantly. Then suddenly remembering something, she dug into the pouch she wore at her side and pulled out two wooden spoons, which she handed to us.

Sadavir tasted the soup tentatively, unsure of what to expect. Unlike the vegetable-rich stews he was used to, this soup was mostly made with dried meat and small tubers of some kind. The soup was very well prepared and soon Sadavir's wooden spoon was scraping the bottom of the bowl. I wasn't far behind him. Nadya smiled as she gathered up the bowls and took them back behind the flap. In a moment, she had rejoined her husband and started asking questions. Unlike her husband, her first concern wasn't with names.

"Where are your parents?" She queried Sadavir.

"They are still at my home, on the far side of the wall."

"Why did you leave?"

"The people there thought me dangerous because I have a Destroyer's stone."

"Are your people so close-minded? In the village closest to us there lives a girl with a Creator's stone. The people there still welcomed her; well, more or less."

"I'm afraid I wasn't so lucky, Nadya." Sadavir's mood had fallen again. Nadya noticed and hurried to change the subject.

"I'm sure you'll like it here. We don't have very much, but we're willing to share." She cast a sharp look sideways at her husband. "It sure beats running around the forest trying to kill one another."

Andre grinned sheepishly. "Yes dear, I know." He turned to us and explained. "I owe it to my wife to note that it was her idea to talk with you. My first plan was call men from the other village and see if we could overpower you with numbers. While you slept, preferably."

Now that the danger was past, Sadavir smiled at the thought.

Chapter 15

History so often judges a civilization by their innovations, their art, or their ruins. This is all folly. If you would know the worth of a society, you only have to look at their most average citizen.
           –Musings of the Historian

"Do you ever think that Olya would be happier if she went to live with the Creators? She does have a Creator's Stone, after all." Nadya directed her question to Andre.

Andre shook his head slightly, but he seemed to be thinking of something else.

"Sadavir, in all your time among the Creators, did you ever see a clear stone?"

"Of course, they're all clear." Sadavir was confused.

Andre shook his head. "I'm sorry, I didn't explain myself very well. What I meant was, did you ever see one that didn't have any color at all, just clear."

"No, never. Does this Olya have such a Stone?"

Andre nodded, his eyes staring off into space.

"I wonder..."

Nadya hit him.

"Now Andre, I don't want to hear any more of your theories. Certainly not in front of our guests." She turned and explained to us. "Andre always has to have a deeper meaning in everything, if he even sees two trees growing too close to one another, he tries to come up with some sort of meaning for it."

"Ok then," Andre surrendered. "I won't make anything out of it, but at the very least I think the two of them should meet, they would have a lot in common, growing up as outsiders in their own land."

"Olya is not an outsider." Nadya objected.

"I know, I know," Andre interjected. "All I'm saying is that she has always felt a little different because of her Stone, I'm sure our young friend here can relate."

Sadavir nodded emphatically. The easy conversation and warm food had put him at ease.

"I would be happy to meet her." Sadavir added.

"Great then, it's settled. I need to talk to their village leader in a few days anyway, you can come along. In the meantime, how would you like to take a look around our village, maybe you can start to see where you could contribute."

Sadavir and I nodded and Andre again took off through the flap of his hut and we scrambled to follow. Outside, as he walked through the open area in the middle of the huts, Andre scooped up a small boy by the feet and carried him, upside down, back to us, displaying him as if he were a turkey on the market.

"This little hooligan is my son, Sasha." The boy, who looked to be about eight years old, laughed. His face was turning beet red.

"Put me down, daddy. I'm getting dizzy." Andre lowered the boy to the ground. The boy righted himself, stood up, and ran off again after the other children.

"Now, I don't want to put any pressure on you too early, but everyone here pulls their own weight, we all contribute to help the village survive. You wouldn't happen to know much about

Creator farming, would you?"

Sadavir shook his head.

"Well, what was your specialty when you lived among the Creators."

Sadavir's gaze shifted to the ground.

"Actually, I was brought up to defend my village against you. Fighting is all I know."

"Hmm, fighting is a necessary skill here, but it doesn't put much bread on the table. I guess you will learn how to do things our way."

Sadavir nodded, then a thought occurred to him.

"Andre, how is it that your people get over the wall?"

"Over the wall? Those spikes are too sharp, I'm afraid, and we suspect your people of poisoning them, so even a small scratch would be fatal. No, we don't go over the wall."

"Then how is it that you raid us?"

"Oh," Andre said, as if suddenly realizing what they were talking about. "Someone opened the gate and let us in, sometimes even told us where the best prizes could be gained."

"Who?" Sadavir was shocked at the treachery.

"I don't know, we didn't exactly stop to ask for his name, he would just randomly open up the door. We just had to be sure we had enough of a lead on your people when we were running back that they couldn't see us close the gate. It's actually fairly tricky business to set that beam up to make it fall into place as soon as the last of us squeezed through and we closed the gate.

"Other times we would simply run off toward the wall, then hide until the mobs had passed and they thought that we had gone over the wall, then we just worked our way back up to the

109

gate." Andre paused.

"Surely your people suspect that someone is letting us in."
Sadavir shook his head.

"Anyways, he hasn't opened the door in a very long time, I
was a very young warrior the last time there was a raid, but we
still keep watch. That is what our sentries were watching for
when you first, umm, met them."

"Do you remember anything about him, anything that
would distinguish him?"

"Well, the only thing I can really remember about him is
that I didn't like him very well, his voice was high and rather
whiny. Of course, you must keep in mind that this was many
many years ago; as I said, I was rather young at the time. Besides,
what do you care now? If we were to shut him down, we would
only be biting the hand that feeds us. We are not great craftsmen;
the only way we can get decent tools is to steal them. This man is
still our best shot at that."

Sadavir shook his head, his loyalties torn by this strange
twist of fate. Andre saw his mental state and directed their
attention to other matters.

"We'll be thankful for a couple more strong backs here in a
little while. We need to move to a different area, we've almost
eaten everything around here, game is getting scarce, most of the
roots and tubers have already been found, and the only nuts left
on the trees are too high for us to get to."

"Too high?" Sadavir asked.

Andre glanced at him. "Hmm, maybe just for us, eh? Well,
you can take a look."

Andre led them over to a nearby stand of trees.

"You see, we can only get nuts from the young trees, the ones that haven't grown very tall yet. The trunks grow long and straight and without lower branches. So when they have already grown tall, we can only wait for the nuts to become old enough to fall on their own, and by then the birds, the squirrels, and the worms have already had a go at them."

I could see what he meant. The trees grew umbrella-like out of the ground, with a long trunk and no side branches until the top. The trunks looked slick and mossy and very difficult to climb. The young ones grew close enough to the ground to allow for harvesting, but the older ones had trunks that held the nut-bearing branches quite high overhead. With the trunks nearly unclimbable, the people could only wait for the ones that fell naturally. Andre continued his narrative.

"We managed to steal some strong rope from your people once and we were able to throw it through the higher branches and pull ourselves up to get some from at least some of the medium-sized trees. But the rope became very frayed and started breaking. No man in his right mind would trust his weight on it now. So, if you can think of another way, go ahead."

Sadavir studied the cluster of trees for a moment, then headed for a tree. I was confused at first, because he didn't head for one of the nut trees, but rather to a very tall conifer that grew nearby. Several children started to gather to watch the spectacle. Monkey-like, Sadavir scaled the tree until he towered above us in the air. The wind caused the tree to sway slightly, but Sadavir's grip was solid.

He climbed until he was very close to the top, even above the nut trees. The children gasped in unison as Sadavir set his foot firmly against the trunk of the tree and launched himself into empty space. The children erupted into cheers as Sadavir caught a branch of a nut tree and swung himself lightly into its high branches. By this time, several adults had also rushed over to see what was happening. The first one to turn to Andre and ask, "What's happening?" was very abruptly answered as a large nut fell on his head. Rubbing his head, the man looked up and was soon dodging other incoming nuts being thrown down from above as Sadavir swung through the nut tree, hanging with ease by one hand as he picked the nuts with his other hand and dropped them to the people below.

The children squealed with delight and ran to get baskets from their mothers. Soon they were frantically gathering nuts from the ground while other children kept a sharp lookout for falling nuts and shouted to warn their nut-gathering companions.

Sadavir drew another gasp from the watching crowd as he finished harvesting the nuts from the high tree he was in and launched himself back into the air to catch at a branch of one of the medium-height trees. He again repeated his monkey act and soon the ground under that tree was also littered with nuts and laughing children.

Finishing the harvest of that tree, he wrapped his arms around the trunk and slid down to the ground to the sound of cheering. Andre came and clapped him on the shoulder.

"That has to be one of the craziest things I have ever seen in all my days. But I thank you on behalf of all the village. Our women take those nuts and can grind them to make a kind of bread that's quite delicious and very filling. It will be an incredible evening tonight, I can tell you that."

Glancing around the village, I could see that he was right.

These people had not been well fed in quite a while. Though they did a good job covering it up, I could still detect the drawn faces and gaunt ribs that spoke of prolonged hunger. Some of the smaller children were already cracking at stolen nuts to get at the sweet meat inside. It made me think of how well we had eaten in Andre's hut. My conscience twinged slightly at the generosity of their sacrifice. After all, I didn't even need to eat.

Sadavir rubbed his sore hands and nodded towards the other trees.

"I can get those some other day. Right now, my hands are tired."

Andre laughed. "Don't worry, you've certainly earned your keep for today, almost every child was able to fill his basket just from the two trees you emptied today. If you can consistently do that, without breaking your neck, you will always have a welcome place in any of our villages, I can promise you that."

"Well, it shouldn't be too hard, I've been doing that sort of stuff since I was eight years old, the difference is that here I don't have a rock tucked between my legs."

Andre looked at him in amazement.

"Umm.." He started, "I have no idea what you mean by that, but I can tell I'll need to hear more about your upbringing. Although I hate to take pleasure in your misfortune, Sadavir, I am very glad that you were forced from your home, because I would never want to go against you in battle or raid a village that you were defending."

The children gleaned the last of the nuts from the ground as Andre, Sadavir, and I turned and walked back to Andre's hut.

For the next couple days, Sadavir was true to his word. Each day, a couple more nut trees were harvested. He never failed to draw a crowd, the novelty never wore off and the people gasped every single time that he jumped from one tree to another. Besides the entertainment, the people enjoyed the variation in their diet from the usual fare of dried meat and tubers. The nuts were sweet and very nutritious.

All of this had an extraordinary effect on Sadavir. For the first time in his life, people were happy to see him, they greeted him warmly as they passed him and held his name in high esteem. Even men who sported bandaged and broken hands from previous fights with Sadavir raised their good hands in greeting.

The children would often ambush him as he stepped outside of Andre's hut in the morning and drag him to the ground. They would all scream and giggle as he would rise from the ground, usually with two or three children still clinging to his arms. He would then pull his arm from their grip with blinding speed. Whichever kid had been holding onto that arm would fall, only to be caught and safely lowered to the ground by Sadavir's foot. His limitless dexterity and speed made him a perfect subject for a thousand games. Sadavir never seemed to tire of any of it as he relived a hundred childhoods to compensate for the one that had been stolen from him.

We had only been there a day when Andre approached me.

"So Sadavir can flit through the trees like a bird and fight like a lion. What special powers do you possess, Sergei?"

I shook my head. "I have no special skills, I'm afraid. But I am fit and can help out with any menial task you would like to assign me. I am all too happy to earn my keep."

"What did you do where you came from?" Andre asked.

"I pumped the bellows for Sadavir's father when I lived with them. He was a blacksmith."

Andre's eyebrow rose ever so slightly. "You dodge questions, my friend; rather well, in fact. I already know that you are not one of the Creators. Neither are you a Destroyer, you are something else. You do not even keep a name for yourself. And there is something about the way you watch my people that makes me very curious about your curiosity. Who are you?"

I could see that I wasn't going to get away with simple stories with Andre.

"I am a wanderer. I keep no name because I keep no home and no family. I watch people and I see their stories and I remember. I am a storyteller."

Andre still didn't seem satisfied with my explanation. "For a storyteller you don't tell many stories. Surely you have many, but you hardly talk at all. How did you even come to this land?"

"I just ended up here. I follow Sadavir because there is something new there, I'll stick around until I see it end."

"Well, storyteller, you must have a lot of time on your hands, because Sadavir has mentioned knowing you when he was just a child. Would you stick around twenty years for a story?"

I didn't answer and the moments grew on to awkwardness. I had met people like this a few times before. There was always one in every place, someone who would see the truth in any lie. The silence swelled and Andre's look of suspicion changed to one of curiosity. A new thought occurred to him.

"Do you age as we do, storyteller? You don't look too much past thirty years yourself, and Sadavir spoke of you as an adult in his childhood stories. Maybe my men were pointing at the wrong man when they started guessing about gods. I'm not superstitious, but something about you just doesn't add up." Andre suggested.

"I am no god." I answered simply. "I am merely a storyteller, as you call me."

Andre studied my face for a moment, trying to read deeper into my soul. Having come to a decision, he clapped me on the shoulder.

"Well then, welcome, storyteller. I hope my people will be deemed worthy of a place in your stories. We can be immortal if we are remembered."

Andre started to head off in the opposite direction, our conversation finished, when something occurred to him and he turned around suddenly.

"Storyteller, do you also like hearing stories?"

I nodded. "Very much."

"Then perhaps you would be interested in our village library."

I froze at the word. Could they actually have a library?

"That would be excellent, Andre." I agreed, trying and failing to hide my enthusiasm.

He smiled. "Right this way."

He led me to a large hut. It was even larger than his chief's hut and I wondered who merited a larger hut and why he was the keeper of whatever books they had.

As we stepped through and I blinked to get used to the darkness, I found that my assumptions had been dead wrong. No one lived here. This was their library. Crude wooden boxes were stacked high and stuffed to brimming with crudely assembled books. I gazed, unbelieving.

116

"Aren't your people nomadic? How do these travel with you?" From just my first glance, I estimated thousands of books resided there. To answer, Andre pulled one of the boxes off the top and showed me leather strap that had been fastened to it, so that it could be carried on someone's back.

"Mostly the children carry them, an individual box isn't very heavy." He started to explain. "Also, we leave a good deal of the books here. The books that travel with us are mostly history books, so that we can keep them updated, and books on religion and philosophy, for those seem to be nearest to the people's hearts. The ones that are left behind are mostly studies, diagrams, theories and plans for inventions."

"Inventions?" I queried. I was used to absorbing vast amounts of information very quickly, but this sudden turn still had my head spinning as I fought to understand it all. "The only person I ever saw invent anything at all was Sadavir's father, but he was very different from the other Creators."

Andre nodded, thinking. "Yes, I would have guessed as much. That would help explain Sadavir's Stone."

I expected further explanation, but Andre just continued to stare off into space, lost in his own musings. I waited a few moments, my curiosity consuming me. I finally interrupted.

"Andre," I started. "I don't want to seem rude or ignorant, but what in the world are you talking about?"

He broke out of his reverie with a smile on his face. "I'm sorry, I forgot that you have been living among the Creators. Maybe you should start in the red section."

He led me to a stand of boxes that had the spines rubbed with red flower petals, creating a dull crimson color on the animal skin bindings.

"These are the histories. They will help you understand the peoples you have been living with. Can you read our symbols?"

I started to nod, but then thought better of it. I had actually learned their symbols quite well, but this was a story I wanted to see through Sadavir's eyes. If I had him read it and tell it to me, I could see his thoughts as he told it. It was his story I was observing, after all.

"I'm afraid not," I responded. "I never really had much of an opportunity with the Creators. Sadavir learned, however, quite well. Do you think the dialects would be close enough so that he could read them?"

"Well, I can't imagine that they would be much different. Creators only ever copied what we started. Did you know that we were once called the Creators?"

I shook my head, hoping that he would explain, but he only pointed at the book I held in my hands, having pulled one from the boxes to look at it.

"You will find all of your stories there." So saying, he turned to leave the hut. He paused at the outer flap and looked back over his shoulder, his face suddenly sorrowful.

"Please do not judge us too harshly, storyteller." Then he was gone.

Chapter 16

Sometimes you find redemption for your sins... and sometimes you burn for them.

-Musings of the Historian

Sadavir was as excited as I was when he heard about the books and he agreed that he would read them and tell me about them as he read.

This plan ended up being very good in theory and downright lousy in practice. As Sadavir started reading, he soon became so totally engrossed in what he was reading that he would hardly even break to eat. Any questions I would ask were answered with dark silence as Sadavir brooded over what he had read. This went on for days as book after book left the boxes in Sadavir's hands. He would read from the morning until it became too dark to see in the night.

I could see that the men would have wanted to get more nuts, since their supply was running low and their wives had returned to serving up pasty soup made from tubers. None would disturb him, however, as his mood was dark and troubled. It was a common sight during those days to see a man's gaze wander up into the trees longingly. His eyes would then wander to Sadavir, he might even start forward to ask about a harvest. Usually by then one of his companions with a bandaged arm or head would pull him back.

There was a certain privilege associated with being a master of violence.

Only a week had passed, however, before Sadavir broke his trance-like study. After a quick foray into the trees after nuts, he asked to talk to me. We walked a ways into the forest before he finally got his thoughts together enough to speak.

"We were their slaves. Or they were ours, I'm not quite sure what I should be calling myself at the moment, Uncle."

"Well, for the moment, let's not call you anything, just tell me what you have learned."

Sadavir spent the next several hours telling me the history of the Creators and Destroyers. He had to stop often as emotions overcame him or he became distracted and wandered off on tangents.

I claim a historian's right at this point to tell the story of these peoples in my own words:

In the beginning, there had been one great source of magic, one man. The history that described the man told it as a myth, as all histories eventually become. Nothing was said about how he gained his fantastic powers, but the reports of them were impressive, even for myths.

The man was a noble sorcerer who wielded almost god-like powers. The tale told of mountains moved, seas called up from the depths of the earth, even volcanic eruptions stopped mid-explosion by the man's uttered command.

His name was Amel.

Amel brought all the people together under a gentle command. For all his impressive powers, he allowed none to worship him or pay him tribute. He said his powers and knowledge were the result of fate, not divinity.

He used his power to serve the people. Everywhere he went, the farms prospered, the wells ran sweet, and disease was cured. It seemed that there was nothing outside his power. In a single generation the people of the land grew from starvation to prosperity, from ignominy to nobility, with Amel as their example.

The day came that Amel decided that his powers needed to be shared with the people. While there were many guesses after the fact, but no one ever truly knew what his intentions were.

Perhaps he was growing old and wanted the people to be taken care of.

Perhaps he thought they were ready.

Perhaps he didn't know it would kill him.

Whatever his reasoning may have been, most commentators agreed on one thing:

He was wrong.

Amel brought all the people together and told them that it was important to work together. He said he would show them how important it was. So saying, he dropped one knee to the ground and held his hand out in front of him, palm open.

As he slowly drew his hand to a fist, light gathered within his hand, shimmering and writhing like a living thing. The myth states that the more the light grew in his hand, the more he seemed to age in front of their very eyes.

As his fist finally clenched, the light had engulfed his entire arm. Just as the light became too intense for any man to look directly on it, Amel thrust his hand to the earth, the light exploding outward like a wave, the ground itself rippling under its weight. It washed over the people in an instant, knocking them all to the ground.

When they regained their feet, all they saw was that Amel had died. The man who had raised them all to dignity lay face down on the cobblestones, his right arm charred and smoking.

The mourning went on for months. Some men gave up hope entirely and died of starvation and despair on Amel's tomb. It wasn't until almost a year later that the first child was born with a beautiful Stone delivered in the same moment. It quickly became obvious that all new babies were being born with the incredible gems. Some were clear, some were opaque, all were beautiful.

It was another twenty years before anyone noticed that those with clear Stones were incredible craftsmen, their Stones would glow when they were truly engrossed in their work. In a dawning realization, people realized that Amel had given the people a great gift. At least, he had given it to some.

Almost immediately, those with clear Stones started to band together to share experiences, to talk about new techniques or simply exult over their good fortune.

If history has shown us anything, it is that when one group combines in status above another group, that other group will combine as well. I suspect it is some kind of innate survival technique when the human animal feels it is threatened.

Their first real war was primal. They were a people who hadn't yet learned sophistication in war. The worst they had known was personal feuds. So now, with an entire people divided against each other in fear and hatred, they learned their first lesson hard:

War is hell.

They battered at each other with rocks and clubs. Farm tools and household implements became instruments in the hands of mobs to crush and cut one another down. When nothing was handy, they would use their bare hands to batter and squeeze the life out of each other.

Amel's people had lost their innocence, perhaps their souls. Although the people were evenly split as far as numbers, the war was far from even. Those with the opaque Stones showed an incredible intelligence and innovation that gave them an edge in every battle. Ambushes, fortifications, and new weapons quickly took a heavy toll on the craftsmen who knew nothing but to charge straight ahead.

As the atrocities on both sides rose in frequency and depravity, fear grew in the craftsmen and hatred grew in those with solid Stones. Once the tide of war had firmly shifted, the end was swift and complete.

The craftsmen were enslaved, forced to use their talents to serve the others, who began to call themselves by a new name:

Creators.

Even as they took the name to celebrate their inventiveness and ingenuity, it only betrayed their deep envy of their slaves, who had been favored with Amel's Gift. Try and train as they might, they would never come close to the amazing skill of those with the clear Stones.

Though built upon slavery, it might have still been a golden age for the people. The brilliant plans and inventions of the new Creators, carried into being by the skilled hands of their slaves, would have catapulted both peoples into an incredible period of technology and prosperity. After all, even a slave benefits when his master rises.

Unfortunately, that isn't how people work. It wasn't long before the Creators found reasons to fight amongst themselves.

Ideological and religious differences soon had them back into civil war. This time the Creators had skilled hands at their disposal to make weapons, fortifications and engines of war.

The days of rocks and clubs were over. Each faction competed against the other not only on the battlefield, but also in the workshop as they ordered slaves to construct better and better means to destroy their enemies.

Elaborate strategies were carried out by trained armies, territories were taken and retaken, and thousands of people died. More battlefields, more fortresses, thousands more died. Ever new weapons, ever new strategies, and thousands more died.

The war lasted for generations. The original reasons were forgotten, replaced by causes of vengeance and dominance. All the while, the slaves grew in number while the masters killed themselves into a minority. Still, the Creators never saw the danger, they only saw larger workforces to help them carry out their schemes.

Finally one scheme came out that was brilliant in its simplicity and incredible in its scope.

A wall.

One side started building it to seal off the other from valuable mines. The other side saw an opportunity to cut off the opposition from their lumber supply. What followed was an ongoing battle more bizarre than any anyone had ever seen. The two armies fought for years at the running edge of the wall. As new sections of the wall were completed, they would simply move their camps and start again.

Neither side harmed the slaves of the other as they both worked on the wall. While it may seem insane, it actually may have been the first sane thing either side had done in decades. At some point the leaders must have seen the wall for what it was: a chance for peace. If the people could not dwell together in peace, they would simply dwell apart. The wall would enforce their cease fire.

Still, while reason may have pushed the peaceful building of the wall, it was not sufficient to stop the fighting. Emotions ran too strong, too many scores to settle. So the violence continued as the massive wall crept its way across the land.

It would be hard to gain adequate perspective on what happened next. In another story, I saw a mirror that showed a person their full life in an instant. Unfiltered, unbiased, it showed a man his true self in a way that couldn't be justified or even defended against. It was a weapon of psychological destruction. Men faced with a realization of that magnitude would crumple like tissue paper under a waterfall.

This is a little like what happened to these Creators. There was a moment when they began to see a glimmer of hope in their madness. That glimmer was the completion of the wall. The violence would end and the people would have an opportunity to live as human beings.

Then the faint glimmer of hope turned to a blood-soaked despair.

The Creators had given no more thought to their slaves than a blacksmith gives to his hammer. They used them as tools, no longer seeing them as human. Unfortunately, their slaves had not forgotten their humanity. They had not forgotten their anger at being placed in chains.

They had also seen an opportunity in the wall, a chance for a new life. They saw a chance for revenge.

The wall reached the cliffs that formed a natural barrier to the land. It had started at the sea, where hundreds of slaves were sacrificed to the ravenous sea creatures to build a foundation in the shallows. It ended now in a split in the land that no climber had ever come close to conquering.

The last thing to be built was a gate. It showed the growing hope of the people, a thought that one day they might even come back together. The fighting amongst the two factions had all but stopped. Only a few lackluster battles still flickered like the dying coals of a fire.

When the last stroke finished the gate, the killing started for real. The slaves had worked out a system, simple but effective. When the completion ceremony was announced, the slaves turned on their masters. It was unanimous and devastating.

The armies were slaughtered as the hordes of workers washed over them. They still lacked the finesse and strategy of the Creators, but it no longer mattered. The wars had dwindled the population until the Creators were outnumbered seven to one. Not a single soldier was left alive. Every commander, general, and strategist was methodically crushed under workers' hammers.

The fate of the rest of the civilization was left up to those they had ruled over. Each slave got to decide the fate of their masters. Cruel masters were killed along with their entire families. Those who were kinder were forced through the gate to the far side as slaves streamed back over.

In just a couple days, the entire race had divided itself like oil and water. They found themselves staring at one another through the gate. The survivors of the holocaust, mostly women clutching frightened children, found themselves with their backs to burning towns and cities, left flaming by the fleeing slaves.

They gravitated to the gate, staring helplessly at the slaves

126

that had massacred their men and now held their fates in their hands. Whether they were looking for mercy, a second chance, or even an explanation, we'll never know. All that is recorded was the statement of the leader of the slaves:

"You have enslaved us, crushed us, all so that you could butcher each other. You are destroyers. We are the Creators now."

And the gate swung shut.

Chapter 17

*One of life's great decisions is whether you want people to admire
you or pity you. You cannot pursue both.*

—Musings of the Historian

As near as I can tell from the other histories, that was over
four hundred years ago. The new Creators lived as they knew
how, no more advancement. The Destroyers scraped by on the
other side of the wall, full of ideas and imagination, but
completely lacking the skill to bring any of their ideas into reality.

"Fascinating." I murmured as I shook my head and
contemplated these new developments. Sadavir had just finished
his rendition of the history of his people.

"Fascinating, Uncle?" Sadavir queried. "I think it's
monstrous. I'm not even sure who the bad guys are anymore."

I smiled in spite of the sadness of the moment. "Sadavir, in
life, there are very seldom good guys and bad guys. Everyone does
what they think is best, they live, they die, and their stories are
told later, their actions judged by strangers."

"Stories told by you, Uncle?"

"Yes, Sadavir, I tell peoples' stories."

"Will you tell mine?"

"Someday."

"Uncle?"

"Yes?"

"Am I a good guy or a bad guy in your story?"

"I only tell the story, Sadavir, the listeners decide that."

He nodded, accepting, and we headed back to the village.

The next day I had the opportunity to talk with Andre about these new developments.

"So I was surprised to learn that the Destroyers accepted such a name from the Creators. It is very rare for a people to accept something like that."

Andre nodded. "It is very hard for people to admit that they are wrong, storyteller. But we are a religious people, there has to be meaning for everything. When our lives fell apart, there had to be a cause. Naturally, at first, it was the evil of the slaves. But as new generations grew and learned of their history, more and more grew to realize how wrong we were for enslaving them and soon the whole people accepted their punishment and the new name that came with it."

"That's good, Andre, that they were that humble, but something still doesn't add up." I probed. "I have seen how people have reacted when they've seen Sadavir and myself in Creators' clothes. There is still anger there, hatred. You can't tell me that those are the eyes of a people who have humbly accepted their fate and their punishment for their wrongdoings."

Andre smiled. "You are right, my friend, things aren't that simple. Everyone of course knows of our ancient sin and of our punishment for it. But, storyteller, knowing that you deserve a lashing doesn't make it sting any less. I challenge you to find a man, woman, or child on this earth who truly wants what they deserve. Besides, that was more than four hundred years ago, the people feel that we have paid our price and they want to see the end of the Creators. Some would even see them enslaved again.

"In the far past there were even splinter groups who tried to go over the wall and retake our ancestral lands, but they were defeated. And each time there was a new attack, the Creators would add to the wall, making it higher, smoother, more dangerous. I'm sad to say that most of their ideas for improving the wall came from memories of the prisons we would throw them in for petty offenses. Now they use our own cruelty against us. I guessed that the spikes and stones are poisoned because our ancestors poisoned the spikes on their walls."

I accepted this information stoically, a lot more things made sense, then something else occurred to me.

"Andre, when you heard me talk about Sadavir's father, you seemed to understand why Sadavir was born with a Destroyer's Stone, why was that?"

"Oh, it's simple enough, storyteller. Even though it was expressly forbidden by old Creator law, there were still some of our ancestors who fell in love with a slave. While it was rare, the result was that a bit of the bloodlines still continue, subdued, in each race. My wife mentioned the first day you were here about the girl who was born among us who has a Creator's Stone. When you mentioned that Sadavir's father was an inventor and a thinker; that was obviously his Destroyer blood in him. I assume his wife was also like him?"

I nodded.

"Well, that settles it, you had two descendants of mixed ancestors get married, and that was enough to have Sadavir born as a pure Destroyer, bits from each of his parents."

We walked for a little while before Andre thought of something else.

"I can't explain the color of his Stone, however, never in my life or even in our histories have I ever seen or heard of such a Stone. We don't know the history of the Creators, but I suspect that they have never seen a Stone like Olya's" He mused.

"Olya?"

"Yes, that is the name of the girl who was born with a Creator's Stone. I think you would like her, storyteller. She is a very interesting young woman. Maybe Sadavir would think so too." Andre winked. I smiled, Sadavir had been here less than a month, and already his marriage was being arranged for him.

Still I worried for my young friend. While Andre was open and generous, it stretched my understanding of human nature to try and believe that all the people would feel the same. Still, Andre was obviously well respected and he was quite determined that Sadavir become one of them.

Andre certainly didn't wait long. We had been there only another week since the revelations of the histories when Andre told Sadavir that he was going to another village in a couple of days and he would like him to come along. Sadavir readily agreed. He smiled and winked as he turned from Sadavir and saw me watching.

"You of course are also invited, storyteller, but somehow I doubt you needed an invitation."

It was indeed a sad day for the kids of the village when Andre left to go to the nearby village and Sadavir went with him. They had lost their favorite toy and playmate.

The journey was a pleasant one. We weren't in any hurry

and Nadya had packed us plenty of dried meat and shelled nuts to eat on the way. As usual, the conversation was mostly between Andre and Sadavir, leaving me free to observe my surroundings. I had always been very fond of the mountains and the Destroyers' land was much more hilly than the plain country of the Creators.

Eventually we arrived in the other village and the other village leader greeted Andre warmly. He eyed Sadavir and me with suspicion, but as Andre explained to him who we were and what we had done for his village, his expression softened and his gaze wandered toward the high nut trees that grew near his own encampment. Andre read his thoughts and laughed.

"Ivan, you always were a conniver. There will plenty of time for that later. As for right now, my young friend came to see Olya, could you call her?"

Sadavir's head whipped around to look at Andre. Somehow Andre had forgotten to mention to Sadavir that he was there to meet a girl.

"I'm afraid that she was summoned to yet another village, a man there was stabbed through the foot by a sharp stick in the leaves and it became infected. We are expecting her back any time now, however, and I would be more than happy to offer you the hospitality of my hut until she returns."

Sadavir's arm flashed to his side with blinding speed and a fist-sized rock broke in two across his armband as he spun to face his attacker. His eyes fell on a young man, several years older than himself, who cursed violently as he crouched, looking for another rock to throw.

"Ivan! How can you stand there while this Creator disgraces our camp?!" The man yelled as his hands raked the leaves on the ground, searching for a rock to throw.

Ivan yelled back at the man, "Vova, this man is no more Creator than you are! Stay your hand!"

Turning to Sadavir, he quickly explained, "Vova's father was killed by Creators. He was already retreating towards the gate when one of them threw a rock and hit him in the back of the head, killing him on the spot."

Sadavir nodded sadly. He understood the bitterness that comes from pain. In the meantime, Vova had dropped his rock, but he still stalked up to Sadavir and extended his hand, palm up.

"Show me your Stone!" He commanded.

"No." Sadavir answered quietly. Andre and Ivan stared wide-eyed at him.

"Sadavir! I really think you should show him your Stone." Andre hissed.

"No, I have been judged by my Stone my whole life. I am finished with it. Vova, I know what you are feeling, I have seen the same feeling in the eyes of my neighbors as they recall their loved ones who fell by the hands of Destroyers."

"Are you calling my father a murderer?!" Vova screamed, his face twisted with rage.

"I'm not calling anybody anything. I stand before you as a man, not a Creator or a Destroyer. If I have wronged you in any way, feel free to try and take your revenge, but if not, I recommend you walk away."

"You profane my father's name!"

"I profane nothing, but you have become like his killers, driven only by hatred."

Vova roared like a wounded animal and swung his fist hard

at Sadavir's face. There was a sickening crunch as his hand slammed into Sadavir's armband, which seemed to materialize in the path of his punch.

If it had been Padam or one of the other Creator youths who had picked on Sadavir in his youth, the fight would already have been over. But this was no pampered youth. Callused hands and corded muscles spoke of a life of hardship. A life like that turns a boy into a man, tough as leather.

Holding his broken hand, Vova attacked again with his feet and knees, showing amazing dexterity and skill as his feet snaked towards Sadavir. His first two kicks hit nothing but air as Sadavir dodged them easily. Vova then gathered himself and launched himself towards the younger man with his knee shooting out, trying to break Sadavir's ribs. The timing was perfect and against any other man it would have been a devastating attack.

Sadavir jumped straight into the air and Vova over-extended his strike right under him. Sadavir landed with both knees on Vova's chest. Vova had already been off balance, the force of the counterstrike drove him to the ground like a sledgehammer. Vova folded up in a way man was never meant to fold. Even as he hit the ground, limbs twisted under him, Sadavir had already landed lightly on his feet. His right arm flashed toward Vova in a finishing blow and his nose broke flat against his face.

Men were already grabbing for weapons to respond to this sudden threat. Things were about to turn very ugly. A beautiful voice broke the chaos.

"What is going on here?!"

"Olya, your timing couldn't have been more perfect, Vova

needs your help." Ivan yelled out. All heads spun to look at whom he was yelling at. A very pretty young lady stood with her jaw gaping open, pretty blue eyes wide and staring. Sadavir, who just a moment before had stood like a god of violence over his fallen opponent, suddenly looked like a small boy again, one who had just been scolded for breaking his mother's dishes. His hands crept behind his back and his toe poked idly into the damp earth.

"Ivan, who are these men? And what are these strange clothes they wear? Are these Creator clothes? What have they done to Vova?" The young lady asked as she walked closer. Ivan hurried to explain.

"This young man was exiled from the Creators, he has a Destroyer's Stone." He turned to look suspiciously at Sadavir. "Or at least, so I hear."

Sadavir grudgingly pulled his Stone from inside his shirt and displayed it. A tiny bit of dark light still rippled across its surface, but was fading quickly. Fascinated, the girl reached out and grabbed the Stone to inspect it more closely. The others chuckled softly as Sadavir was pulled over by the cord around his neck.

"Umm, I could take it off if you would like."

"Oh!" The girl realized what she had done and let go of the Stone as if shocked. This time it was Sadavir's turn to smile.

"Really, it's ok." He said and pulled the cord over his neck and handed her the Stone. For a comparison, she pulled her own Stone out of a leather pouch at her side. Just as Andre had said, there was absolutely no color in it, but was as clear as crystal. Olya's gaze was fixed on the black Stone, as if trying to unravel some mystery. It was Ivan that broke her reverie.

"Umm, I don't mean to interrupt, but Vova is still in a great deal of pain. Olya, could you please help him?" Ivan insisted, pointing to the man who still lay on the ground, holding his broken hand and breathing shallowly. I guessed that he had landed hard when he fell down and now sported some broken ribs to match his broken hand. Both Olya and Sadavir turned to look down on him, almost surprised to see him there. Sadavir looked suddenly sick for having been the cause of his suffering. He handed her Stone back to her.

"I hope he will…" Sadavir started feebly, but was suddenly distracted by a faint glow that came from her hand. Olya noticed it too.

"Whoa! Did you see that?" Sadavir nodded the affirmative. She had transferred both Stones to one hand to fish in one of her pouches for some herbs and the Stones had reacted. She opened her hand and they both stared at the spectacle contained in her palm. White light seemed to pulse back and forth between the two stones, even the blackness of Sadavir's stone seemed to emanate the white light.

"Mmm…" Vova groaned from the ground. "…feels better."

Olya looked from the Stones in her hand to her patient lying on the ground. She reached her hand slowly toward Vova's broken hand. The closer she got, the more his face, distorted by pain, relaxed. As her hand came to hover directly over the broken hand, the Stones shone brighter and I could actually see the bones of his hand form back to their natural state. The flesh on his skinned knuckles smoothed and healed in moments before my very eyes. In just a few moments, his hand looked as good as new. Even scratches that couldn't have been caused by his fight with

Sadavir faded and then disappeared altogether. She moved the Stones over his ribs and in no time at all, his breathing was even and deep. She pulled the Stones back and they dimmed. Vova sat up and stared at Olya.

"Thank you." He murmured, at a complete loss for words. Similar shock was evident on the faces of everyone present. Sadavir and Olya exchanged looks, stepped over Vova, and knelt down over a plant that grew at the base of a tree. Seeming to almost read her thoughts, Sadavir reached and bent the plant over, breaking the stem so the plant barely held together. He then sat back and Olya leaned forward with the two Stones clutched tightly in her hand and held them over the broken plant. The Stones glowed again and the plant righted itself and the stem solidified, as if it had never been broken.

"Can I try?" Sadavir asked in a voice so low it was almost a whisper. A reverent hush had fallen over the gathered audience. If anyone even understood what was happening, they certainly couldn't yet wrap their minds around the implications.

Olya nodded and handed him the Stones. She leaned forward and broke the plant's stem again. Sadavir stretched his hand out to the plant.

A surprised yelp escaped Olya's lips as the plant was completely obliterated in a burst of dirt and juicy green shrapnel. Sadavir opened his hand and instead of white light, the same dark fire I had seen dance on the Stone before seemed to dance over the clear Stone, which in turn fed the black fire and returned it back stronger to the first Stone. Sadavir dropped the Stones as if his hand were burned. The two Stones fell to the ground where they quickly dimmed. His head dropped into his hands.

"I am truly a Destroyer, that is all I can do."

Without even thinking about it, Olya put her arm around his shoulders and whispered that everything was going to be all right. They remained there for some time, a statue of despair and sympathy. Sadavir finally raised his head. His upbringing had allowed no room for self-pity; he wouldn't let it rule him now.

He picked up the Stones from where they had fallen and placed them tenderly in her hands.

"I want you to have my Stone. You can do far more good with it than I can."

She nodded, humbly accepting the gift. The rest of us stood enthralled, observers in a moment of lost emotions.

There they stood, looking at each other and the Stones she held for almost a full minute before Andre broke the spell.

"By the way, Sadavir, this is Olya; Olya, this is Sadavir. Ivan, Vova, you can close your mouths now."

Chapter 18

After careful consideration, I have decided to be an eccentric.
-Musings of the Historian

That night we slept in Ivan's house. Not much was said,
everyone seemed to be absorbed in their own thoughts. The next
morning was much more jovial, especially when Sadavir took to
the treetops and the children of Ivan's village were able to fill
their baskets with nuts and proudly present them to their mothers.
Olya gasped even louder than the children as she watched him
jump from one tree to another. As he made his final jump and her
gaze was fixed on him, I looked down at the hand she held by her
side, both Stones were clamped tightly together in her fist.

Andre finished his business with Ivan. It was mostly
logistics about the coming migration. They agreed that when the
time came to move their villages, they would move together for
safety and companionship. Their business concluded and the nut
trees harvested, Andre became anxious to return home and we
started out that same day. Even Vova turned out to wave us
goodbye and wish us a safe return journey.

I noticed that Sadavir took a great many backward glances.

We had only traveled a few hours before a boy from the
village we had just left came running up to us, out of breath.

"Come back." He blurted out between breaths.

"Now then, take your time and tell us why we need to come

back, little one." Andre said.

The boy took a few gulping breaths and finally gasped out, "A boy fell and hurt his head. Real bad."

"Well, can't Olya help him?" Sadavir asked.

The boy shook his head. "She says the Stones aren't working and she needs you to come back."

Sadavir and Andre exchanged glances.

"Well, I think you should go back, Sadavir, but I'm going to keep on pressing on home, I'm already missing Nadya."

Turning to me, he said, "You can either go back with him or come with me, Sergei, you're welcome either place."

"I'll go with Sadavir." I replied. He nodded, and after clasping hands, we parted. The boy, seeming to have endless energy, resolved to run back to the village ahead of us and tell them that we were coming.

Sadavir stumbled over a root and I had to catch his elbow to keep him from falling. I raised an eyebrow, it may have been the first time I had ever seen Sadavir trip since he had learned to walk.

"Do you have something on your mind, Sadavir?" I asked.

"No." He denied. Then he seemed to think of something and smiled. "Not really something, more like someone."

"Olya?"

"Come then, Uncle, who else could I possibly be talking about? Wasn't she wonderful?"

"She is certainly a special girl." I admitted.

"Have you ever been in love, Uncle?"

I walked in silence as Sadavir searched my face with his eyes.

"Once, Sadavir. Just once." I responded softly, and something in my tone ended the conversation and Sadavir contented himself with floating over the ground next to me.

When we entered the village a couple of hours later, we were greeted by running children, who grabbed Sadavir by his hands and dragged him through the village to a small hut on the outskirts of the village. As we ducked in Olya was holding the hand of a young boy, who appeared to have taken a very bad knock to the head. The skin had split open and the boy was unconscious.

Sadavir walked into the room and almost instantly a faint glow could be seen coming out of Olya's right hand. She smiled at Sadavir and passed the Stones over the boy. The wound closed and color returned to the boy's cheeks. When she finally pulled her hand back, the boy sat up, rubbing his eyes.

"I'm hungry." He said. I reached into my pack and gave him a handful of shelled nuts, which he accepted and consumed in a matter of seconds. He jumped off the table and started to run outside, hearing the laughter of other kids. He paused at the door and turned back.

"Oh yeah, thanks." He said, and then was gone out the door.

Sadavir and Olya smiled at each other.

"I'm sorry you had to come back, they wouldn't work when you were gone; there wasn't any light."

"It seems that the power of the Stones is tied to the people who bear them." I mused, almost to myself.

"I guess you need to stay with me." Olya said, then suddenly blushed, realizing what she had said. "I.. I didn't mean…"

"Don't worry about it." Sadavir said, blushing profusely

himself. Olya recomposed herself and rephrased her comment.

"I meant, it would be good if you could stay here for a while, other people need help."

"Of course," Sadavir stammered. "I'd be happy to help out."

Olya smiled warmly at him. Sadavir blushed a deeper shade of crimson.

"So, Sadavir," I started, interrupting the awkward silence that ensued, "Perhaps you and I should see to some sleeping arrangements."

"Oh, yes, of course. Umm, Olya, would you know of anywhere we could stay for a little while?"

"Well, let's go ask some people."

Strangely enough, it ended up being Vova who offered us room and board. He still didn't fully trust Sadavir and I suspected that his main motivation for having us stay with him was to keep an eye on us.

Vova was a bachelor who lived alone. Both of his parents had died, and he had inherited their hut and property. He had plenty of empty places for us to stay in. Our gratitude for his hospitality dimmed a little that evening. To move from Lauria's cooking to Nadya's had been a fair drop, but to eat what Vova served us was almost more than I could stand. How that man grew to be that strong eating that food was beyond me.

Dinner was eaten in absolute silence. Vova had nothing to say to either of us; and, for our part, it took all the concentration we could muster to keep all unfavorable expressions off our faces as we chewed and swallowed methodically.

The mood changed for the better after dinner. Vova pulled out a long wooden flute. He raised it to his lips without preamble or explanation and began playing. Although the flute was poorly made, Vova handled it with a master's touch. Sadavir was enraptured. They had music among the Creators, but it was loud, artless, made for dancing and drinking.

The tune Vova played was sorrowful, hypnotic. It made you want to weep and cheer, while at the same time, holding you completely breathless, not even daring to move, lest the spell be broken.

The last haunting notes hung softly on the air, then faded away as Vova lowered the flute to his lap.

"That was incredible!" Sadavir exulted. "That was the greatest thing I have ever heard! Can this be learned? Can you teach me?"

The first smile I had seen from Vova spread across his face. Any artist will revel in sincere praise, no matter the source.

"Oh, it was just a simple tune. Don't you have music where you come from, Creator?"

"Not like this." Sadavir impulsively reached out his hand and Vova handed over the flute.

"May I?" Sadavir asked, pleading.

Vova's smile melted. But it was obvious that certain rules of hospitality applied to this situation.

"Very well." He grunted, grudgingly.

Sadavir raised the instrument to his lips and blew. Vova's somber countenance instantly erupted into laughter at the tortured sound of the instrument. He reached across and pulled the flute away from Sadavir, still chuckling.

"Well, that was a fine first lesson, Creator. They really don't have music where you're from, do they?"

Sadavir, embarrassed at his botched attempt, shook his head.

"Well, well, I never thought I'd pity a Creator." Vova said.

"I'm no Creator." Sadavir responded.

"You lived with them, you grew up with them, you're just like them, Creator."

"I am NOT!" Sadavir's tone had sudden taken a sharp edge. Vova became serious again. His left hand drifted to close over his right, an unconscious reminder of his hand breaking earlier that same day.

"Easy there, I really didn't mean anything by it. If you're against the Creators then you're in the right spot, I didn't know you felt like that about it."

Sadavir cooled down a bit. "It's not really like that. I don't hate them. A lot of them are actually really good people, most of them, in fact. There's just a few who have no honor, who let hate and fear rule their lives. I will never be like them."

Vova fidgeted. He knew perfectly well that the same accusation had been leveled at him. His eyes dropped to his lap and he saw a way out of the uncomfortable silence. He held out the flute.

"Here, Sadavir, how about I teach you to play?"

Sadavir smiled. "I would like that."

It was good to see Sadavir actually have a friend. Of course, Vova once again took second place in Sadavir's thoughts when the next day dawned. Olya was all that occupied Sadavir's mind. For the next few days, they took turns being one another's shadows, finding the tiniest excuse to be together. Having discovered her new power with the two Stones, she seemed intent on curing every ill of every villager. Sadavir, of course, had to attend.

For his part, Sadavir took to the trees every chance he had and made sure the village did not begrudge his presence among them. Naturally, Olya had to be one hand, ready to heal Sadavir should he fall. Every day the children of the village would lug baskets of nuts home to their mothers. Sadavir and Olya would walk along behind. Sadavir would carry Olya's basket as the two of them escorted the children back to the village.

They were a fun couple to watch. Constantly embarrassed and stammering, having the time of their lives.

I was confused then, a few days later, when Sadavir again became very sullen. Not even the cheery company of Olya could pull him out of his reverie. If anything, her presence seemed to make things harder on him. Something was eating him from the inside out, I could tell. I was content to wait until he opened up to me and told me about it, as he always did. Olya was not so patient, however.

We had been in Ivan's village exactly one week and Ivan had asked me to help him repair his hut. It had gone well. Ivan was a hard worker. It was easy to see, however, the difference between the two people I had lived with. Aric had always worked in smooth, powerful actions; he was confident and skillful. Ivan, on the other hand, relied solely on determination. His hands were clumsy and he struggled with even the simplest of tasks. His hands were large, meaty, and scarred. They fumbled with the small fibrous rope that held the pole framework of his hut together. It was no surprise that he needed help, if for only the purpose of holding the poles as he tied and retied his fat knots.

It was almost sunset before we were finished. Ivan thanked me heartily and I turned my steps toward Vova's hut. Olya emerged from behind a nearby hut and called out softly to me.

"Sergei, can I talk to you?" Her tone was pleading.

"Of course," I responded. I looked around to see Sadavir, not expecting him to be very far from her. He was nowhere to be seen, however. My ears caught the sound of an awkward tune being played on a flute in Vova's hut. Sadavir wasn't with her.

"What's the matter, Olya?" I asked.

Now that she had my attention, she suddenly seemed ashamed to have called out to me.

"I was actually hoping you could tell me. Aren't you Sadavir's uncle?"

"No."

Her look was confused.

"Then why does he call you that?"

"Because he has known me as his uncle from his earliest memories, but I'm really not of his people."

"Oh." She said, not really knowing how to carry on from that point.

"Umm, Ivan calls you Sergei, but Sadavir says your name is Amar. Which is really your name?"

"Neither."

The corners of her mouth pulled down even farther as her brows knits together. The conversation was flying far from what she had planned.

"Well, what should I call you?"

"Call me whatever you'd like, Olya."

"Well what are you?" She asked, exasperated.

"I'm a traveler, a wanderer."

"Well, if you spent twenty years with Sadavir's family, you must not be very good at it."

I smiled widely, she had spunk.

"You may be right, Olya, I'll try to work on that."

"I'm sorry, I just got a little upset. But seriously, what should I call you?"

"Well, why don't you just call me what Sadavir calls me?"

"Do you mean 'Uncle'?" She asked, her eyebrows raised.

I nodded. She paused thinking it over, then she smiled.

"I would like that. Uncle."

"Uncle it is then." I agreed. "So what was it you wanted to ask me?"

"Oh yes," she started. "I was wondering if Sadavir had told you anything."

"About what?" I asked. Suddenly this fiery girl who had stood up to me just a short while before was now biting her bottom lip and fidgeting with her hands.

"Well, I just thought, kind of like... you know when we..." She glanced about at nothing, lost for words.

"Anything about you?" I prompted. She nodded. Even in the pink glow of the sunset, I could see a red blush creeping up into her cheeks.

"It's just that he's been so upset recently. I don't know what he's thinking, if maybe he's upset with me or something. He didn't even come find me today; he just stayed inside and practiced on that infernal flute. He's getting much better, by the way." She added grudgingly, not above feeling a little jealousy for the crude instrument. "So I was just wondering if maybe he had told you anything."

"No, he hasn't, Olya. Although I am fairly sure that he isn't mad at you."

"How can you be sure?"

"I can be sure because I know Sadavir. If he were mad at you, you would know it. He gets that from his father, he has no compulsions about telling someone how he feels. They've come up with some fine speeches, I have to say." I commented.

"I wish I could meet his parents." Olya said.

"Maybe one day you'll get the chance, Olya."

"Do you really think so, Uncle?"

I nodded.

"I wish I knew him a little better." Olya said.

"Maybe I can help with that." I offered.

"Could you?" She pleaded, the eagerness showing plainly in her eyes.

"Certainly, is there someplace we could sit down?"

"Sure, follow me, there is a bench outside my hut. Families often sit there when they bring someone for me to heal."

When we were comfortably seated outside her hut, I launched into my narrative. I have seldom enjoyed such an attentive audience. It was like giving a man on a sinking ship a lecture on swimming.

"Sadavir is no Creator." I started. "But neither is he a Destroyer. He is a man with a strong sense of loyalty, but no one has ever accepted his loyalty. He has a strong sense of duty, but no one has ever allowed him to serve.

"His father, Aric, is one of the finest men I've met, and he loved the boy with all of his heart. His mother, Lauria, has always been his kindest friend. Everything Sadavir knows and everything

he is came from just those two people. They gave him everything
he needed to survive, except for one thing: they never taught him
to hate."

Chapter 19

There is no greater man than one who feels personally
responsible for the whole of mankind.
                  -Musings of the Historian

"Uncle, what in the world are you talking about?" Olya
interrupted. "Why would Sadavir need to hate?"

"In truth, he doesn't, but that does leave a gap in his life. He
has been hated almost his whole life. No man can endure that
without asking why. Most men will respond by hating back. This
is the way of the world, it's human nature. But Aric and Lauria
never let Sadavir hate them. Sadavir was never allowed to lose
himself in that hatred. So, as I said, that leaves a gap."

"What kind of gap?" Olya asked when I paused.

"Purpose, Olya; every man, woman and child has to have a
purpose. Even those who believe in no higher power still reach for
some reason to explain their existence. If he had been allowed to
hate, then Sadavir would have had a purpose, to hate, to take his
revenge on those who had hurt him, and to fight against them.
Instead he was made their protector."

"Shouldn't that have then become his purpose, Uncle?"
Olya asked, her brow again furrowed. "Why couldn't he accept
that as his purpose?"

"Because he was denied that purpose by the same people
who he would have protected. He still needs a purpose, Olya."

She started nodding slowly. She had the simple intelligence of the Creators, but in her, it came across as innocence, an ability to see things at their purest form.

"But Uncle, now he is here with us, he is the only one who can harvest the nuts off of the high trees, he helps me to heal people, he does so much good now, can't he define himself in that?"

I shook my head.

"As good as that is, Olya, it is still not enough for Sadavir. He has seen too much injustice, he has thought too deeply, he needs some higher purpose to account for all of that. And truthfully, beyond that, that boy was born for glory. Even though he might not want it or even avoid it if he gets the chance, there is still something of greatness within him. When a man squelches his own potential, he loses something of himself. Sadavir needs to do something great, to be something great. Nuts won't do it, I'm afraid."

"I think I understand now, Uncle. But I'm afraid I don't see how I can help."

"Well, that will all tell in time, the future is still and always will be a blank page. However, now you must pay for your story."

Olya looked stricken. "I, uh, have nothing. The village takes care of me. Maybe Ivan…"

I raised my hand to interrupt her.

"I was thinking more of a trade, Olya; a story for a story? I would very much like to hear yours."

Olya sighed deeply.

"Certainly, Uncle, but why would you want to know about me?"

"Call it an old man's curiosity."

Olya scoffed. "Old man? You don't even look as old as Ivan, Uncle. Don't start telling me more stories, I only have one to pay you back with."

"Ok then," I smiled. "Let's hear your story."

"What would you like to know?"

"A wise man once told me to always start at the beginning, and to stop when I reached the end." I quipped. "Who were your parents?"

Her head lowered.

"I don't know."

"Are they dead?" I asked softly.

"I don't think so."

"Were you abandoned?"

"Not really."

"Umm, perhaps I should let you tell the story, Olya." I offered.

"It's not so funny when it goes the other way, is it, Uncle." She jibed. "But very well. I am the only one anyone's ever heard of that was born with a Creator's Stone.

"So, when I was born, they held a council to decide how they would handle me. Was there something like that for Sadavir too?"

"Sure, something like that, please go on."

"Anyway, they decided that I would either be a great asset to the people, or a very great danger. So, they decided that the best thing to do was to sort of pass me around."

"I beg your pardon?" I interrupted. "You'll have to explain

that a little bit more."

"You see, my parents kept me for a couple of months, then another family took me in for a couple of months, and so on, changing every couple of months. I've lived in almost every village on this side of the wall.

"That way, if I were to be an asset, then everyone would get a chance to benefit from it. And if I were a danger, then the hope was that I would be more attached to the people, like everyone was my family, understand?"

"It seems a little bit calculating for deciding someone's life, but before I pass judgment, I should ask you what you thought about it, growing up like that."

"It really wasn't all that bad. There isn't a village this side of the wall where I couldn't go and find friends. And when I got old enough, they gave me my own hut and let me live wherever I wanted."

She paused, thinking.

"But...?" I prompted.

"Well, it would have been nice to have a real family, I have a lot of friends, but I was never able to get really close to someone, and now the situation is just getting a little confused, if you know what I mean."

I shook my head. "I'm afraid I don't."

"Oh yes, forgive me, Uncle. I forgot for a moment that you aren't from these lands. In our culture, the father arranges the marriages. If the father is dead, then the mother decides. If both parents are gone, then the leader of the village chooses. But for me..." She trailed off.

"But you have neither parents nor a village or village

leader." I filled in.

She nodded. "Life is very hard here. If a woman isn't married while she is still young, she won't be able to have children to continue the generations. All of the girls I knew growing up are married now. Several have children already. I am becoming an old maid and no one even cares because I am the healer."

Her voice had taken on a very bitter tone.

"Why should I need children of my own when I get to care for so many. Just like why should I need a family of my own. Uncle, I want a family."

Her voice broke on the last sentence and she buried her face in her hands. I put my hand reassuringly on her shoulder.

"It seems to me that the choice is now yours, Olya."

Her head lifted and she sniffed back tears.

"What do you mean, Uncle? Who will arrange my marriage for me?"

"Your village leader."

"Oh, Uncle, you don't understand. Ivan isn't really my village leader, he really hasn't even known me that long. How could he…"

"I didn't mean Ivan, Olya." I interrupted.

"Then what did you mean? Please, no more riddles."

"You have your own hut. You are the one who decides where your hut goes. You are the one who chooses how you will live."

"So?" She asked.

"Olya, you are your village leader. Arrange your own marriage."

"Uncle, that is the dumbest thing I have ever heard."

I laughed and patted her knee. "You just think about it."

"Ok." She agreed. "But how would I go about it?"

"Well, how would a village leader go about it?"

"First, he would discuss the match with the boy's parents and with whoever was taking care of the girl. If they agreed, then both the boy and the girl would be brought into the village leader's hut and he would inform them of the match. They would then get a chance to talk and plan out their life under the supervision of the village leader. He also gives advice on what works and what doesn't. He gives advice on how to be happy in a marriage and so on."

"Ok then, Olya, it sounds like you have a pretty good idea of how to get things rolling."

Olya shook her head, but she was smiling. "Uncle, you are truly a strange man."

"If you'd believe it, I hear that a lot."

Olya and I parted and I had the feeling that while she still thought my view on the matter was crazy, she didn't much care. I had given her the possibility that she could have Sadavir for her own. She would have accepted any story that had that ending, no matter how crazy.

Unfortunately for her, Sadavir found his purpose before she had found her courage to approach him about marriage. He blurted it out to me one morning over another tasteless breakfast in Vova's hut.

"I have to go back." He stated simply. I just nodded. I had suspected that he would come to that sooner or later. And after all, I was only there to see the story. Telling Olya ten minutes later was not nearly so smooth.

"What? Why?" Olya demanded, not understanding this sudden change in events and Sadavir's sudden change in mood. "Go back to where?"

"Back to the other side of the wall."

Olya gasped. "But they'll kill you! They hate you, why would you go back?" Her tone was pleading.

"Because the people were never meant to be separated like this. The Stones and the people were meant to work together. Amel knew it from the beginning." Sadavir almost seemed to be surprised at the words coming out of his mouth.

"Maybe, but I don't see why you…"

"Look at your people." Sadavir interrupted. "They suffer without the power of the Creators, and my people will never realize their true potential without the help of your people. What is going on right now is wrong, and I can't sit by and let it happen."

"Then I am going with you." Olya decided.

Sadavir opened his mouth to object, but could find no words. He knew that the surest way of winning over his people's hearts was through a demonstration, and the kind of demonstration he could give would only drive more fear into their hearts. He needed Olya with him. After a few moments of opening and closing his mouth, looking rather like a fish, I thought, he nodded.

"But you must always listen to what I say and obey very quickly, your very life might depend on it."

She nodded meekly, a strange pose for her as she had struck me earlier as quite an independent young woman.

156

"Uncle, I cannot ask you to come with me."

I smiled. "What are you suggesting? That I stay and miss the end to the story? I could no more stay than you could."

"Do you think that it will be the end of the story, Uncle?"

"Maybe, maybe not, a lot will depend on the hearts of your people. Judging from what I've seen so far, I would guess that this story will not end soon, but that you will be there at the end, whatever it may be."

Sadavir nodded, asking for no further explanation. Olya looked as if she wanted to ask a million questions, but felt uncomfortable about questioning me.

"When did you want to start?" I asked.

"As soon as possible." Sadavir responded. Now that he again had purpose, his old determination had set in and he couldn't rest until his new task was completed. Turning to Olya, he asked. "How long before you can be ready to go? And could we possibly trouble your people for some extra supplies."

Olya thought for a moment, then spoke. "I think I might be able to put it together in a day, would you mind sleeping at Vova's again tonight?"

Sadavir shook his head, after all, there was no real rush, he was just anxious to be on his way.

While the light still held, he was able to harvest a couple more trees that were located a bit farther from the village, followed by a small army of basket-bearing children and even a few curious adults who had missed the show earlier because they had been out hunting. On his last jump from tree to tree, his hand came down wrong on a branch and the broken stump punctured his hand. He was able to slide down the tree without any problem and once back to the village, his hand was quickly healed under the glowing light held in Olya's gentle hands. He looked up into her eyes as she held his hand for just a moment longer than needed for the healing process. She lowered her eyes and released his hand, quickly jumping up to complete her preparations for the morrow.

The morning came all too quickly and again we found ourselves walking through the forest on a dim path. Sadavir's step was quick and determined, and both Olya and I had to hurry to keep up. It was only when Olya stumbled over a rock somewhere around midday that Sadavir started to slow down and take occasional breaks.

It had taken us about two or three days of idle wandering and another half day to reach Olya's village originally walking from the wall. But with the new pace that was set by Sadavir, the wall could already be seen in the far distance as the light started to fail and Olya insisted that they stop and build a fire.

"You'll be in no shape to handle yourself if you starve and exhaust yourself." She scolded, though I noticed that she was the first to sit and pull off her shoes and gently rub her feet. Sadavir, who seemed to have as much energy as when we had started in the morning, set off into the brush to gather firewood for the night's fire. He wasn't gone long before he returned with an armful of dry sticks and dead brush, good for starting fires. He dropped it on the ground and headed back into the brush, this time after bigger logs, I guessed.

I dropped to my knees and started to arrange the kindling and dry brush to start a fire when Olya pushed me to the side.

"Hey now, this is woman's work. Leave it to the men and

the chances are fairly good that they'll burn down the whole forest."

I smiled, she wasn't far off in her estimate. Men were very intelligent, but they could only be intelligent at one thing at a time. It was easy to for a man to become distracted and forget about something as small as a fire.

It wasn't long before she had scraped out a small pit and lined it with rocks. Her small hands moved expertly as she arranged the brush and sticks. Her tinder was dry and caught fire quickly as she struck sparks into it with a piece of flint and the back of her knife. The fire was just starting to burn nicely as Sadavir returned with an armful of larger logs. These he also deposited by the fire and headed off into the brush again for a second load to last through the night.

Olya started to prepare a light supper.

"Sergei, how long have you known Sadavir?" She asked me.

"Ever since he was born, I lived in the house of his father."

She looked confused. "Just how old were you when you came to live with them? You don't seem a great deal older than Sadavir or myself."

"I started wandering when I was still very young." I offered, not a whole truth, but she accepted it and continued her questions.

"What is your craft, Uncle? You don't seem to be a warrior like Sadavir, and you have no Stone that I can see."

"In truth, I have no craft. I have spent most of my time as a common laborer. While I lived with Sadavir's family, my craft was the skillful pumping of the bellows and the intricate removal of scrap metal."

Olya smiled at my jest. She opened her mouth to ask another question, but at that moment, Sadavir walked back to the fire and deposited yet another armload of wood beside the fire. He then settled himself on the ground staring hungrily at the small iron pot that Olya was slicing tubers into. I guessed that the pot was made by a Destroyer, since the workmanship was rather shoddy, obviously just trying to get it to hold water and little else.

The little pot got the job done, however, and soon a delicious smell filled the air as Olya's stew boiled on the red coals. Olya finished hers first and sat for a moment, staring at Sadavir's arms.

"What do these symbols mean?" She asked, pointing to the inside of his armbands. She had noticed the small marks that had been etched into the steel, one on each arm. "I'm afraid I never was very good at deciphering symbols."

Raising his right arm, he pointed with his left hand at the small mark on his right armband.

"This one means love." He reversed his arms and pointed to the other.

"This one means honor."

"Who made them for you?" Olya asked.

"My father." Sadavir answered simply. We were all bedded down for the night before Olya asked her last questions.

"Sadavir, have you ever taken them off?"

"No."

"Will you ever take them off?"

"When I know I'm safe."

She asked no more questions and the quiet music of the mountains soon sang us all to sleep.

The next day Sadavir awoke us early; he had already started a fire. Olya set about making breakfast, while Sadavir fidgeted and paced.

"We should be able to make the village by nightfall." He said, more to himself than to anyone in particular.

"Wait, won't we still have to travel a long way to get to the gate?" Olya asked.

Sadavir smiled, his first one of the trip. "No, I know of another gate, much closer to here. A secret gate." He winked at Olya playfully. She responded by looking perplexed.

Gulping down breakfast, we set off again, Sadavir again at a fast pace. The wall slowly grew in our eyes until we stood next to it. I was again awed by the craftsmanship that went into its construction.

"Umm," started Olya, "I don't see any gate here, Sadavir."

Sadavir smiled roguishly. "Oh, you just need the right key. Could you possibly lend me your Stone, Olya?" Her eyes widened as she realized what he meant to do. She handed him her Stone and walked quickly away from Sadavir and the wall. I followed her lead.

Sadavir turned and faced the wall, both Stones clutched in his right hand. He took a deep breath and then with a quick movement, thrust his fist at the wall. The wall in front of him seemed to distort for a flash of a second, then the wall burst outward in a blast of dust and rock fragments.

Bits of rock fell around his head and shoulders, but he didn't seem to notice as he watched the dust settle and listened to the rubble click and clatter. For the first time, he seemed pleased with his ability to destroy. He stepped back, the dust swirling behind him and spoke to Olya.

"See, I told you there was a gate here."

Chapter 20

I shudder to think about what this says about me personally, but there are few things that thrill me more than a tragic coincidence.
–Musings of the Historian

As we neared the village, night was already falling. Sadavir paused and lowered himself to the ground out of sight of the village.

"I think we had better stay out of sight until we can talk to my father." He explained. "I don't think the people are going to be really happy about seeing me. No need to start any trouble until we absolutely have to."

Olya and I also laid ourselves down next to Sadavir and we all lay there in silence as we waited for the night to provide us cover. Sadavir fingered the symbols on his armbands; Olya fingered the Stone in her pouch; and I watched the two of them.

At last Sadavir tapped my arm and we walked quickly but quietly to the outskirts of the village and worked our way to his house. Not a single light burned in the house as Sadavir approached the door. He opened the door and slowly slipped inside. Olya and I started to follow, but before we could, we heard a clang of metal on metal and a scuffle within. Olya and I rushed in to help, but inside the house, it was pitch black and all we could do was close the door behind us so as not to draw any unnecessary attention. The sounds of struggle ended and there were some whispers that I couldn't quite make out. After a moment, sparks jumped into a lantern and the room was thrown into sharp contrast as the dim light revealed Lauria standing in the center of the room with the lantern. The lantern was quickly set on the table and she rushed the embrace Sadavir.

I looked around the house. Something was definitely not right. Stepping over the iron pot that Lauria had thrown at Sadavir, I stepped back to survey the room. A chair was tipped over and a few dishes had fallen off the table. If I had guessed I would have said that Aric had stood up very quickly from dinner, throwing his chair backward and knocking most of the dishes from the table. Sadavir voiced the question that stood foremost in my mind.

"Where's papa?"

Tears streamed down Lauria's face as she sobbed out,

"They took him." She then broke into deep sobs and could say nothing more. Sadavir looked absolutely lost and confused, a warrior not knowing where his war was.

Olya jumped into action. She brought Lauria a chair and sat her down. She told Sadavir to find some blankets and cover the windows. Olya put an arm around Lauria and held her as she cried. Sadavir returned with the blankets and with my help soon had all of the windows covered. Olya took an extra blanket and stuffed it around the crack at the bottom of the door. After she had blocked all of the outer openings, she walked to the lantern and, with a bit of fiddling, soon had it burning brightly, lighting the whole room quite well. She spotted some candles and lit those as well. The whole house was bathed in a warm, yellow light. Olya then busied herself cleaning up the house, righting the chair, retrieving the thrown pot, and taking the fallen dishes to the kitchen. This had a pronounced effect on Lauria and she stopped crying to stoop and help Olya clean up the dishes and take them to the kitchen.

The whole process only took about five minutes, but Sadavir had already started pacing again, like a lion in a cage. Worry was etched deep on his face. Lauria reentered the room with Olya. She sat down and composed herself, wiping her tears away with both hands.

Now that she had gotten over her hysterics, she took a moment to clutch Sadavir to her, holding tight to her only child. When she separated herself from him, she sat down in a chair to relate her story. Olya pulled up a chair next to her and kept an arm around her.

"It's Saddhan." She started. I saw Sadavir's fists clench at the name.

"They came and took Aric away. They called him a traitor." This time I was confused.

"How exactly did they take him?" I asked. Aric was worth ten of them with his massive arms and his courage. He wouldn't have gone willingly and if they had taken him by force, there would have been a lot more signs of it.

"When Sadavir left, Aric threw out all of his training equipment. Saddhan stole one of the launchers off of the ramps. He went to another blacksmith in another village and had him make more of them, with larger levers and three strips. He also changed them so that they would launch small stone balls."

Lauria's voice trembled as she recalled the memory.

"He took control of the village, he killed Boran."

I remembered Boran, he had been the old man who had offered a compromise when the mob threatened to kill Sadavir as a child. He was a respected leader among the people.

"What have the people done about it?" Sadavir asked, already knowing the answer.

"Nothing." Lauria spat. I saw Aric's fire and disgust at his people's cowardice now reflected in his wife's eyes and voice. "Most of them have been won over by Saddhan's words and plans. The others, those who would object, didn't have the courage to stand up to him. Only Aric publicly came out against him. They took him this morning. I think he was going to fight them anyway, but Saddhan turned the weapon on me and told Aric that I would be killed if he didn't cooperate.."

Sadavir's arms quivered and his eyes had turned cold.

"Where did they take him?" He asked.

"They've converted Saddhan's cellar into a kind of prison. They added a heavy locked door and lined the walls with stone. All the stone masons helped, it was done in a day. Saddhan wanted him killed, but everyone else wouldn't have it. They insisted that imprisoning him would be enough." The stress and worry of the day was starting to catch up with Lauria and her whole body looked fatigued. Her eyes started to drop.

"Olya, could you stay here with my mother? I'm going after my father."

"No chance, Sadavir, I'm going with you, what if your father needs to be healed, or what if you need to use my Stone? I have to be there."

"I don't care, Olya, I'll figure it out. You have to stay here."

Although already half-asleep, Lauria raised her head and

166

smiled sleepily. She squeezed Olya's hand and fell asleep entirely. Sadavir lifted her easily and carried her to her bed. Returning, he resumed his argument with Olya.

"I will not allow you to come and I won't hear any more from you about it."

I smiled, this story I knew well. Its ending was certain.

"Well, Sadavir, I'm going to the city square, whether you like it or not. All you get to decide is whether I'm going with or without you."

Sadavir gripped his hair in exasperation. Turning to me, he asked.

"Do all women manipulate men like this?"

"Yes, but they are usually more subtle, Olya is just learning." I chuckled.

"Fine then, you can come with us, but you must remember to do exactly as I say exactly when I say it, agreed?" Sadavir offered.

"I promise." Olya said.

Our odd threesome worked its way through the village to the town center. It wasn't hard to find Saddhan's house. It was built higher than the ones surrounding it and had a guard posted outside. Sadavir didn't waste time with strategy but simply started walking toward the guard.

"Hey, who is that?" The guard called out. "You'd better stop, this will kill you, I promise."

"I will shoot!" the guards voice grew more frantic as the dark figure drew close to him. Finally his shaky finger pulled the trigger mechanism. The guard couldn't see what had happened. The night shifted around the dark figure and the stone ball he had fired burst into dust just in front of the intruder. In another second, Sadavir had closed the distance between them and knocked the astonished guard unconscious. Olya and I followed.

"Uncle, we need to find out who else is left inside. If we…" Sadavir whispered, but was interrupted by loud laughter that sprang from the darkness. The voice I had heard a few times too many. Saddhan.

"I thought that there might be a rescue attempt, but I never expected to see you, Sadavir. May I just say well done." Saddhan's high voice scratched the night air.

Saddhan stepped from the shadows surrounded by several others, all held the new weapons. The men represented Saddhan's inner circle. If he gave the order to fire, it was certain they would.

"I guess we have you to thank for these, Sadavir. Quite nice, although your father was too stupid to see their true potential." Saddhan mocked.

"Olya, get behind me!" Sadavir hissed. This time, she didn't argue but darted behind Sadavir's back.

"Oh, that's very nice, very noble of you, Sadavir." Saddhan was truly enjoying his moment of victory. "Now, after seeing what happened with that guard, I might actually guess that you might be able to block these stones. That means you might be thinking of fighting us all. There's just one glitch in your plan." Saddhan paused and drew a deep breath before yelling at the house.

"Padam!"

"Yes, father?" The voice came from inside the house.

"If you hear sounds of a scuffle out here, or if I yell again, I want you to kill Aric, is that understood?"

The voice inside laughed. "Perfectly, father."

168

"So, what's it going to be, Sadavir? You might be able to escape with your lady friend, but your father and your outsider friend are going to die unless you cooperate. Frankly, you already know what I would prefer, your family and your friends have been a disease in this village for too long."

Sadavir trembled with rage, but with his father inside the house, the bands on his arms might as well have been shackles. His arms dropped to his sides.

"Now, if you would be so kind as to walk into the house. The pretty girl can stay out here with me for a moment."

Sadavir's arms snapped back up.

"Uh uh uh. That's non-negotiable, Sadavir, I need to keep an insurance policy on you, and that little girl seems to be my best bet. Don't worry, I'll send her in as soon as you are in the farthest corner of that nice little room I have fixed up for you down there."

Sadavir truly had no choice. His head hung low as he and I walked into the house, down some stairs and to a heavy locked door. The guard that stood outside of it opened the door and Sadavir and I were pushed in. Aric caught his son as he was thrown in and held him by the shoulders staring at him, not fully believing his own eyes.

Several guards leveled their weapons at Aric while Olya was brought down and thrown in with them. As soon as she was in, the heavy door swung closed and I could hear the heavy bolt on the other side fall into place. There were no windows, so the room fell back into blackness.

Chapter 21

I have seen so many ordinary men do extraordinary things when they are fathers that it no longer surprises me. They simply have too much to lose.

-Musings of the Historian

"Sadavir, what on earth are you doing here?" Aric's voice rumbled low out of the darkness.

"I found out something incredible about the Stones, papa, I needed to come back and tell the people."

"What about the Stones?" Aric asked, his predicament momentarily forgotten as his insatiable curiosity was piqued.

"Well, when Olya and I combined our Stones, their powers complemented each other, she was able to heal people almost instantly, whereas my 'gifts' were magnified as well." Sadavir's voice still held bitterness.

"Wait, who is Olya?" Aric sounded confused.

"I'm Olya." Olya's voice sounded out of the blackness. "It's nice to meet you."

"Nice to meet you too, Olya." Aric responded. There was an awkward pause in the darkness.

"Is she pretty, Sadavir?"

I smiled, I could almost hear Sadavir blushing.

Aric laughed loudly at his own joke, a welcome sound.

When he spoke again, however, his tone was grave.

"It's good to see you again, son, but you should not have come back. And you shouldn't have tried to rescue me."

"Would you have done any different, papa?" Sadavir challenged.

"Maybe not, but there are much greater things at stake now than any one man's life. You were the last hope of the Destroyers, ours too, for that matter."

"Papa, what are you talking about?" Worry had wormed its way into Sadavir's voice. I had seen Aric in a wide range of emotions, from happiness to rage, but this was the first time I had heard despair in his voice.

"Your little spat with Padam and his friends along with the twisting of my devices into deadly weapons provided Saddhan with the exact shift of power he needed. He has had over a hundred of those things made, the other blacksmiths' smithies have burned almost non-stop since you left. Tomorrow morning, an army leaves from here to cross over the wall.

"Sadavir, they are going to kill all of the Destroyers."

Olya gasped in the darkness

"They couldn't..." She started, the fell silent.

"I was hoping that you would be able to stop them, Sadavir. Only you have the speed and the wits to stand against them. Now, I just don't know." Aric's voice had dimmed, a great man brought low.

Olya's breathing had become irregular and I could tell that she was crying.

"Is there no way out of here?" She asked.

"Maybe with the right key." Sadavir responded.

"Could you blow down the door?" I asked.

"No," Sadavir responded. "Well, I guess what I mean is that I could, but I'm not ready to yet."

I understood. Sadavir had seen the guard waiting outside the door. With the power of the combined Stones in his hands, that door and anything outside of it, including the guard, would be utterly destroyed. Sadavir was ever ready to fight, but he had not yet killed.

"So what did you have in mind?" I asked.

"When everyone leaves in the morning, the house will be empty, I can blow a corner off the house and we can escape that way."

"Sadavir, no. We're underground; you would bring the whole house down on us. Not even your black Stone and armbands could save us from that." Olya protested.

"Maybe, but maybe not. If I did it in the corner while the rest of you were in the other corner, there's a good chance that there will only be a partial cave-in."

"Right on top of you!" Olya was adamant. "There is no way you're going to do this."

"I hate to interrupt a good argument, but what the devil are you two talking about?" Aric asked.

"Sadavir wants to use both Stones to blow a hole in the roof and bring the roof down on himself. Stupid boy, trying to be a hero. What are we supposed to do then? We are still unarmed and alone."

"She does have a point, Sadavir." Aric added, also in no hurry to have his son martyred. "Saddhan will be sure to leave plenty of guards behind to keep the town under his thumb.

172

Furthermore, three people can't do much against an army, you're no good to us injured or dead."

"Heal me." Sadavir blurted out, the idea striking him suddenly. "Olya, you can heal me, just get the Stones out of my hand and heal me. Then I can deal with the guards."

"It's too risky, Sadavir, I don't think you should do it." Olya's voice pled softly, but she had run out of counter arguments.

"I agree with her." Aric chimed in.

"Ok, then, I'm waiting to hear a better plan." Sadavir's voice had an edge to it. "Because it seems like the current working plan around here is to sit in the dark and wait while Saddhan butchers an entire race of innocent people. Is that the plan we're going to go with?"

Only dark silence answered him.

"Ok, then, risky it is, but I'm doing it. Now let's all get some sleep, tomorrow will be a full day."

No one answered him. There were some sounds of movement as everyone tried to find a space to sleep in the cramped quarters. Eventually, everyone quieted down, but I doubt that anyone got much sleep that night.

At long last, we started to hear some motion outside. The muffled noises grew to include shouting from several people. Saddhan's shrill voice could be heard above all the others, shouting commands.

It seemed an eternity before the noises started to dim and Saddhan's commands faded in the distance. Eventually, they could not be heard at all. After waiting a few minutes, I could hear Sadavir start to move around.

"Ok, everyone, I'm at a corner, all of you move away from

173

my voice until you get to the other corner."

It didn't take long, since it was a rather small room. Olya and I sat down in the corner and Aric placed himself protectively over us both.

"Ok, be ready." Sadavir said.

Looking toward where his voice came from, the darkness seemed to ripple and shift for just a moment, then it seemed as if the whole world had exploded. In what sounded like a crack of thunder, the stones above Sadavir were suddenly gone, and for a fleeting moment, he stood alone in the sunlight.

In the next moment, the stones came tumbling down on him, his arms raised above his head. The bulk of the stones and earth smashed into Sadavir like a large fist, crushing him to the ground. The whole structure shook, but held, only a few stones fell from the ceiling above us. One of them dislodged just above us and fell, bouncing off Aric's broad back.

No sooner had the sound of thunder subsided than Aric spun around, searching for his son as the sun shaped pillars in the swirling dust. I could see blood on Aric's back, the falling stone had broken the skin under his shirt. He didn't seem to notice though, as he threw rocks almost as big as my torso to the side as if they were made of balsa wood. He brushed the last of the rocks aside and grabbed onto Sadavir's hand, which still clung to the two Stones. He pulled Sadavir from the pile of rubble. He quickly pried Sadavir's hand open and handed Olya the two Stones.

"Heal him!" Aric pleaded desperately.

Olya needed no encouraging as she crawled over the rubble to hold the two Stones over Sadavir. Sadavir's breathing was shallow and sporadic, blood ran over his face, mixing with the dirt and rock fragments. More than anything else, his body just looked wrong, bending in the wrong places and in the wrong ways. Sadavir's body was broken.

Aric looked anxiously at Olya's hand, but the two Stones remained dark. Aric looked frantically up at Olya, who looked like she was about to be sick.

"His Stone is linked to him." She explained, suddenly remembering what they hadn't planned for. "He also needs to be concentrating for them to work."

I was shocked as Aric's hand snapped out and slapped Sadavir across the face. Sadavir's breath jumped at the stroke. Again and again Aric's heavy hand rocked Sadavir's face. Sadavir's eye's fluttered.

"SADAVIR!" His father yelled at him, their faces not two inches apart. "Wake up, son! You need to think about your Stone." Aric's voice was firm and commanding, it had almost as much effect on Sadavir as his striking hand had. Comprehension slowly filled Sadavir's dreamy eyes, followed quickly by pain that threatened to steal his consciousness again.

My eyes darted to the open hole above us. I could hear running footsteps coming from afar. The guards that had been left behind were coming quickly, and we stood defenseless.

"CONCENTRATE!" Aric yelled again. Sadavir's eyes refocused and the Stones in Olya's hands started to glow faintly. The glowing grew brighter as Sadavir's wounds started to mend together.

"Don't move!" the yell came from above as the first guard peered over the gaping hole, his weapon pointing down at them, he was soon joined by the second, who was breathing heavily from the run over to the dungeon. Both held their weapons ready, panic and confusion playing across their features.

Aric started to stand up, slowly, his arms in plain view.

"You, girl! Stand up!" The guards ordered. Olya did not move, but continued her task as the last of Sadavir's bones and wounds returned to their normal form. I could hear more footsteps coming, walking now. I saw Sadavir's hand, hidden by Olya's body, sneak up to her hand, still held over him, and pull his own black Stone from her hand. The rest of him remained motionless until he had his own Stone clutched firmly in his hand.

Sadavir's arms lashed out and roughly threw Olya to the side, under the rest of the house and out of view of the guards. They swung their weapons from Aric to Sadavir and fired. His arms flashed and the stones burst into dust against the tempered steel of his armbands. In his clenched fist, I caught a small glimpse of his stone and the darkness that swirled wildly on its surface. Both men dug frantically in pouches by their sides for more ammunition.

Sadavir rolled into a crouch. With drying blood and dirt still caked on his face, he made for a truly demonic sight, anger etched deep in his features.

He sprung out of the hole, pulling himself easily over the edge and into the sunlight. One man was trying to pull back the lever on his weapon to fire it. The other gave up on trying to load it and swung the weapon like a club at Sadavir. Both weapons hit the ground at almost the same time as Sadavir hit both out of the air with his armbands, the mechanisms smashed and useless. His arms flashed up and two more stones, fired by the other guards who were still running over, were smashed against his armbands.

His hand snaked out and grabbed one guard, thrusting him

back off his feet and slamming him hard to the ground. From his crouched position he sprang at another guard and simply knocked him over the head with an armband. The guard crumpled to the ground even as Sadavir put a foot to his chest to leap over him at the last two guards.

The two guards turned and ran for cover. Sadavir was on top of them in moments, throwing them to the ground from behind. Watching the scene, I was reminded of a lone wolf taking down a running deer.

The guard who Sadavir had left conscious pulled his weapon from the ground and finished pulling the lever to arm the weapon. He lifted the weapon to aim at Sadavir, who was busy finishing off the other two guards.

His weapon fell from numb fingers as Aric's massive hand grabbed the man's wrist and squeezed. Tears welled up in the man's eyes and he dropped to his knees as Aric's hand clamped down on his wrist as he would on a pair of blacksmith tongs. Aric gave an extra little squeeze, then shoved the man hard onto the ground, where he remained, holding his wrist and whimpering.

Aric turned and pulled Olya and myself out of the hole. Once out of the hole, I looked around to see what had become of Sadavir. The two guards that had run were lying unconscious in the dust, but Sadavir was nowhere to be seen. My eyes flickered to the row of houses, where three guards were peeking around the corner of a house to aim their weapons at our little trio. Suddenly I saw an extra pair of arms, these wearing armbands, flash from behind the men. Shouts of surprise and pain were heard for a few more seconds. Then all fell silent.

Chapter 22

There are few things more powerful than ideas, and words are the shapes of ideas.

–Musings of the Historian

Sadavir walked out from behind the house.

"I think that's all of them." He said. Aric nodded. I looked toward the rest of the village. All around us were starting shouts of surprise and alarm. I could see men picking up clubs, picks, and shovels and forming into small groups. I shook my head. I was getting rather tired of these village mobs.

"Son!" Aric said, grabbing Sadavir by the arm. "You don't have time to deal with these right now. You need to go find a way of stopping that army."

Sadavir paused a moment. He knew his father was right, but he didn't want to leave him to the mob. Aric apparently had come to the same conclusion I had about Sadavir's feelings. He smiled.

"Don't worry about me, son. I don't think these will be any trouble." As he spoke, he swept up one of the fallen weapons off the ground, pulling the lever back easily. He reached down and picked up one of the pouches the guards had carried and tucked it in his belt after fishing out a stone. He dropped the stone in the firing groove and nodded to his son.

Sadavir shook his head, but turned and started running out

of the village. Olya ran quickly to the other places where the guards had fallen and retrieved the fallen weapons.

"Why isn't he heading toward the gate?" Aric wondered out loud as he watched Sadavir run to the south. Olya smiled.

"Oh, there's another gate, Sadavir's gate. I think he means to get to the north gate ahead of them." She replied.

"You mean there's another gate?" Aric's confusion showed openly on his face. The confusion turned into an understanding smile, however, as his eyes strayed to the shambles of a house that lay behind them. A new thought occurred to him.

"Olya, if there is another way out of here, I think you should go." Aric said. His tone made it clear that it wasn't a suggestion. Olya bristled.

"Now, why would you send me away? I can fight beside you just like Uncle here could. Is it just because I'm a…" She stopped herself short, an idea occurring to her. Without another word, she turned and ran in the same direction Sadavir had gone, her long legs speeding her out of the village. Aric nodded.

The mob was getting closer, but moving very slowly. Aric leaned down and loaded another weapon, holding one in each hand, pointed right at the leaders of the mob. It wasn't surprising to notice that Padam, although not walking in the front, provided the loudest voice to the mob. Why he had been left behind in the first place, I didn't know.

"Kill the traitor!" If anything, his shrieking voice was even higher than his father's. "They are going to warn the Destroyers, they'll kill us all!"

Aric's disgust was plain on his face and he answered the charges, his thundering voice drowning out Padam's squeaky

179

protests.

"I am no traitor!" He boomed, "You have all known me for all of my life. I have always been fair, no man has ever been turned away from my door hungry. Have I ever harmed any of you?"

The crowd shifted uneasily and Aric continued, answering his own question.

"No! It is you who have attacked me. It is you who have threatened my family, tried to murder my child. Who here is traitor? Who here has turned against their own?"

"Your son is dangerous, the people were right to act." Padam's voice echoed angrily from the back of the crowd.

Aric didn't answer his attack, but rather smiled.

"Oh yes, and who did my son attack? I tell you no one. I say that he was attacked and he defended himself and his friend."

"My friends and I weren't doing anything!" Padam shrieked.

"And who is it that speaks?" Aric addressed the crowd, ignoring Padam. "The son of a weasel. We have all been to their store and bought their wares. Who among us hasn't been lied to and cheated by them? Who among us hasn't felt the injustice of their lofty looks and their inflated prices? Who is this jackal that calls my son a liar?" Aric's face was red and caked with dirt and his voice shook the crowd with its volume and intensity. The entire crowd unconsciously shifted backwards, away from the thundering mountain that bore down on them with his words.

"Think of Saddhan. What do you think he'll do once he has slaughtered the Destroyers? Do you think that he will return here and life will return to normal?" Aric paused for just a moment to let the people think through what he had said.

"He will make slaves of us all! For years we have felt his love for power, for years we have felt his contempt. Through your fear of the Destroyers, you have given him an army. You have created your own master."

Each person in the crowd looked at one another, but no one seemed to know what to do. A few dropped their weapons and walked away, but the bulk of them stood their ground, unconfident, but resolved to see the matter through.

"So be it." Aric said grimly. He sat down on the ground and aimed both weapons at the crowd.

"You might as well get comfortable." He announced. "Because I am going to sit here and wait for my son to return. The first person to move gets shot. And you already know what these things are capable of, Saddhan proved that when he killed a defenseless old man."

"Only two of them are loaded!" Yelled Padam. "Let's rush him! Move!"

The crowd didn't budge.

"You're a pretty big hero from the back of that crowd, Padam." Aric said, "But it's the people in front who need to move, and none of them look all that anxious to die."

"He can't kill us all!" Padam shrieked. "Get him, you cowards!"

"I have enough to kill you, Padam, and one other person. I'm not seeing anyone volunteer to escort you to your final end. Also, there's the little problem of what they're going to do after I've killed you and they've rushed me, many more are going to get their heads knocked in before I go down, I promise you that. Now shut up, you little pipsqueak, or I will shut you up."

Aric's voice had become menacing and he shifted his
weapon to point at Padam's face. Padam yelped as he saw the
action and ducked behind the others. He didn't talk anymore. One
of the braver ones in the lot spoke up, a stone mason named
Baldev.

"And what happens when your son returns, Aric? What's to
stop you from killing us all?"

"The same thing that stopped us from killing those guards
when we had the chance. The same thing that Saddhan lacked
when he murdered Boran. We are not murderers, Saddhan is. The
Destroyers are people just like you and me. What they do, they are
driven to do. And we are the ones who drove them to it!" Aric was
yelling again.

Several in the crowd had become angry again, twisting
their weapons in their hands.

"That's not true!" Shouted one.

"The Destroyers are animals! Their Stones are evil!"

The crowd rippled dangerously, Aric had struck a nerve.
Too many people had lost loved ones to hear what he had to say.

"And who said their Stones are evil?" Aric roared back. "My
son has discovered that the Stones are to be used together. The
people were never meant to be divided! I have seen with my own
eyes the power of the Stones when they work together. It is
beyond anything any of us have ever seen before! If we ever are to
realize our true potential, we must forget the wrongs of the past
and work with the Destroyers to build our future, for our sakes
and for theirs."

"They killed my brother!" One voice screamed, wrenched

with fury and pain. Others murmured assent. Others yelled out their own reports of loved ones killed or crippled by the Destroyers.

"And they will kill your children if we don't act!" Aric answered, rising back to his feet. "The killing will continue if we don't act to make peace. The madness must end!"

"The madness will end!" Padam's voice reemerged in the argument, although he still hid his face from view. "We don't need that vermin! And the killing will be ended when my father has killed them all! Even if what you say is true, it is meaningless. Give up, blacksmith, or die when my father returns."

Aric smiled. "Oh, I don't think so, Padam. My son is going to intercept your father and his misled army. Maybe it will be your father who will need help before this is done."

"Your son is still only one man, Aric. He can't face an army. We are even getting more people from other villages." Padam sounded unsure.

"We'll see." Aric responded, settling himself back down onto the ground. His voice was confident, and only I was close enough to see the worry in his eyes.

Most of the mob contented themselves to do the same, resolved to wait it out. Several remained standing, looking at Aric with hate in their eyes for the words he had spoken against them. As the hours passed, however, even they grew tired and slumped to the ground, deciding that they could glare at Aric just as well from the ground.

The day wore on many of the mob had fallen asleep under the warm sun. Aric let those who had left earlier bring food and drink for everyone. Some objected or even threatened them when they also brought food to Aric and myself, but they paid them no mind. Some even voiced their encouragement of Aric and expressed their hopes that Sadavir would fare well.

Dusk was beginning to set in when tired footsteps were heard approaching. Aric's head whipped around to see Sadavir trotting in. He smiled widely. Several in the crowd got to their feet, but still no one dared to move.

"He'll slaughter us all!" Padam wailed.

Sadavir trotted in, out of breath.

"Papa, we need to go."

"Did you fight the army?" Aric asked, confused.

"No, there were even more of them than I thought, there's no way I could block a volley by that many weapons. I jammed the gate, they won't be able to get through without tools, I suspect that they will camp there tonight and send someone back in the morning for tools, none of them brought anything but weapons. Olya found me, she has a plan. But we need to leave now, there is much to do...

"...and we need help." Sadavir finished, looking up at the villagers. Aric nodded. Turning, he addressed the crowd, both those who sat hostage and the others who had gathered around when it became known that Sadavir had returned.

"Who among you is willing to fight for your freedom? I promise you that if Saddhan is allowed to carry out his plans, none of you will ever be free again. Come! Join us and help us stop him before things get any worse."

There was a long, awkward pause, then a man stepped toward them, he had been one of the first to abandon the mob. I had seen him in his woodworking shop, his name was Faisal. He was soon followed by about five others. Padam was furious.

"Traitors! Scum! I will see all of you killed! My father will hear of your treachery! Your families will curse your..." His voice trailed off as Aric's weapon shifted slightly to point at him.

Some of the men suddenly looked uneasy. Faisal spoke their thoughts.

"What about our families?" He asked.

"Bring them with, they will be looked after, I promise." Sadavir answered.

Aric nodded to Sadavir.

"Go get your mother, son, she'll be worried." Sadavir nodded and ran off again. The men also ran off to retrieve their families and whatever supplies they could grab at a moment's notice. All the while, Aric's untiring arms held the weapons on the hostile crowd.

As many of the men returned with their families, they picked up some of the other weapons dropped by the guards. The waiting crowd became a lot more docile as Aric's two weapons pointed at them turned very quickly into seven. Once everyone was gathered, we started to back out of town. Once they had a good head start, they turned their backs and walked quickly out of the village.

"Don't be too anxious to follow us!" Aric shouted over his shoulder.

Indeed, most of the people who rose slowly from the ground looked like they only wanted to trudge home to a warm meal.

When we had traveled out of sight of the village, I put my hand on Aric's shoulder.

185

"I'll catch up, leave the door open for me."

Aric looked confused.

"Where are you going?" He asked me.

"I'm going back to the village. I need to see another part of the story." I stated simply.

Aric merely shook his head.

"You are a strange one, Amar. Just get back as soon as you can."

I nodded and turned my feet back toward the village.

Chapter 23

The first step of any successful plan is to plan.
—Musings of the Historian

Night had already fallen by the time I returned and the square was abandoned. I hid myself in the remains of the fallen house and waited for morning.

The suns first rays were beginning to peak over the far mountains when I heard the unmistakable clatter of an approaching army. I left the rubble and worked my way over to one of the other buildings. I was sure that the broken building would be Saddhan's first stops. I was right.

The army filled the town. Sadavir had been right; it was indeed a vast army for this people. Saddhan obviously had pulled from all the villages on the Creators side and the army easily pushed five hundred men strong, all armed with the new weapons. From what I had seen from the Destroyers' villages, each village could have mustered a maximum of about thirty fighting men on short notice. It would have been a slaughter.

No sooner had the army entered the town than Padam came running to meet his father, yelling, even at a distance, the news.

"They escaped! Aric held the whole village hostage and they escaped!" Saddhan cursed bitterly and spat on the ground.

Saddhan started giving orders to the villagers, ordering

them to gather their tools and follow him to the gate to break it down.

Baldev, the one who had stood up earlier from among the crowd, approached Saddhan and spoke.

"Saddhan, several of us believe that there should be a representative appointed, by vote, that should go with you and counsel with you concerning your decisions with the army. It is our futures too, after all."

Saddhan viciously backhanded Baldev across the face. Baldev reeled from the blow and raised a hand to his bleeding lip.

"I will not allow my actions to be questioned!" Saddhan screamed. Composing himself, he shouted out to the villagers, who looked on with wide eyes. "If there are several leaders, it won't be long until we get too tied up in our own bickering that we lose our effectiveness. We need to be able to act quickly, and that means a strong central leadership. Do you want your children slaughtered by Destroyers? I certainly don't, so we must be strong and act now."

Not pausing to see what effect his words had, he resumed yelling orders. When no one moved, he grabbed a weapon from the man standing next to him.

"What is wrong with all of you?!" He screeched. "The Destroyers will kill us all, and now we finally have a chance to destroy them and you balk. Well, perhaps I'll have to convince you of how serious the situation is."

He then grabbed Baldev, who still stood in front of him, fingering his torn lip. He whipped him around and kicked at the back of his knees, causing him to fall into a kneeling position in front of Saddhan. He held his weapon up to the back of Baldev's head.

"Now move! I don't want to hurt anyone, but if I must take one man's life to save hundreds, I will make that sacrifice. Move!" He screamed. This time he got results. The people sprang into action, gathering supplies and tools. Baldev, rather than writhing in fear, seemed to be trembling with rage. A tribute to the personal courage of the man, he rose from his knees and turned to face Saddhan. The weapon was pointed straight at his chest, but Baldev started to yell at Saddhan as if he didn't even notice the imminent danger he was in.

"Aric was right! You are the villain here, not the Destroyers! And I will die before I spend another moment on my knees while you…"

There was a sickening thud as the stone fired from Saddhan's weapon and tore through Baldev's chest. Baldev coughed hard, pulling hard for breath. He sunk to his knees and fell over in the dust. The whole village was silent, watching. As Baldev's breathing slowly stilled, Saddhan grabbed another weapon from a nearby soldier.

"Are there any more traitors in our midst? Let them speak now! Our people can never be strong if we allow such lies to be spoken to tear at our very core. No one? Then be quick about your preparations, we must leave immediately."

"Father, if I may?" Padam's squeaky voice spoke at Saddhan's side.

"Yes, son?"

"They didn't go by the gate, Sadavir was the one who blocked the gate from the other side, they went to the south. I think there is a hole in the wall there, we can catch up to them faster going that way."

"Good work, son. You serve your people well." Saddhan said proudly.

The final preparations were made while a nameless woman wept quietly next to the still Baldev.

Just as the blue sky has still not lost its magic and wonder, the tears of grief in the eyes of a new widow have not lost their horror in my mind. How many such tears had I seen in my wanderings? More than I liked to remember. The causes and the many reasons for those tears had long been forgotten, however, and only the agony of the moment remained.

Pain always outlasted causes. The scars always outlived the crusades.

Such were my thoughts as I raced along, just out of sight of the army. I had stayed as long as I could, then ran out of the village, trying to circle my way around the army so that I could reach the hole in the wall before they did. I almost succeeded.

I had almost reached the wall when I was spotted. A chase ensued and already I could hear stones hitting behind me as I approached the wall. Lauria's face appeared in the hole in the wall, her hand beckoning to me frantically to hurry. In my detached way, I wondered what plan they had to stop this army once I was through the hole.

My wonderings soon had their answers as I stepped through the hole. Only two women stood there, Lauria and a woman I had not met before, a Destroyer. Lauria raised her hand, which held two light blue Stones, her own and the Stone of the nearby Destroyer. The stones shone with a pale blue light and the stones that littered the ground started to shift and move. Just as the army grew near enough to be firing stones through the opening, the opening closed. The stones shaped and fitted so tightly together it was as if they had formed there from the birth of the planet. Lauria smiled triumphantly. After seeing her son and husband taken from her, she now held the power to stop an entire army from threatening her family. It was a good day for Lauria.

"I'm glad you made it. Hurry, we must join the others." We turned and walked away from the wall to the sound of Saddhan's vehement cursing from the far side.

Lauria's course took us directly north. We traveled for most of the day before I saw the reason why.

A staging area had been set up around the north gate. The Creators had set up some crude shelters there and a few of the women were bent over small fires, fixing an evening meal. We weren't the only ones arriving in camp.

"Sergei, good to see you again!" Ivan boomed. He was walking into the camp from the east as we walked in from the south. He was followed by several of his fighting men, including Vova. I was surprised to watch as Vova approached Sadavir and greeted him warmly. The others also moved through the camp greeting old acquaintances from Andre's village, who were already there.

For the most part, the Creators watched on, openly uncomfortable and afraid in their new circumstances. They had chosen to follow Sadavir and Aric, but a lifetime of living in fear of Destroyers couldn't be overcome in a mere moment of decision.

For their part, the Destroyers reacted to the Creators' presence by acting as if they weren't there at all. They had come to fight off a threat to their home; that was all they cared about.

I wasn't surprised to see Olya at Sadavir's side. He had finally found some time to wash the blood from his face and he looked a good deal more human than when I had seen him last. He was talking to some of the other Creators, but he broke off their conversation abruptly when he saw us approaching.

"Where is the army?" He yelled out to us even as he was walking to meet us.

Lauria answered for our small group.

"As of this morning, they were at the hole in the wall. We sealed the hole and I think they will now head north to the gate."

Sadavir nodded. He then paused, then nodded again, this time more to himself. He took a deep breath and turned around.

"Everybody listen to me!" He announced. His voice was shaky and I smiled. Even the most confident man in battle can fall apart when faced with the horrors of public speaking. Sadavir seemed to understand his role fairly well, however. He was the only one who was known and somewhat trusted by both peoples, if something were to be done, he would have to start it. He stepped up to his task with determination.

"The army is going to be at that gate tonight or in the morning, we have to be ready. To do that, we must work together."

Several of the Creators nodded, while the Destroyers, for the most part, looked disinterested. They had fought with the Creators before and saw no reason to worry. The Creators were cowards. Sadavir grabbed one of the launcher weapons from his father.

"This is what they will be carrying, more than four hundred of them!" So saying, he turned and fired at a nearby tree. The hard stone imbedded itself deep within the trunk. Suddenly the Destroyers looked more alert.

Ivan was the first to speak.

"Sadavir, we know what power you hold when you hold both Stones, can you destroy this army and save our people?" His tone was hopeful.

"Yes, Ivan, I can." Sadavir's eyes flashed as dark as the Stone that hung around his neck. "I can butcher them all in their tracks. I can then walk through the carnage and carcasses and face the crying eyes of their wives and the wails of their children as they go hungry in the night. Is that what you would have me do?"

Ivan's eyes dropped to the ground.

"What choice do we have?" Yelled Vova. "We did not ask for this war! We did not ask for any of this! What would you have us do, Sadavir? Our wives still wait for us at home, our children still need their fathers. What of them?! Would you have us face down their weapons? Are we your sacrifices that you may be merciful to your own?"

Vova's voice choked with bitterness, but he still listened for Sadavir's response.

"I'm saying that we should find a way so that no children will cry tonight." Sadavir responded simply.

"And how is that possible? If there is a way, please tell us now." This time it was Ivan that spoke.

"Gladly. Papa, if you will." Aric nodded. Andre stood next to him, grinning idly.

"Vova!" Sadavir called out. "If you would, could you please pick up a rock and throw it at me."

"Again?" A rare smile crossed Vova's face as he

remembered their first meeting.

Sadavir smiled in return. "Yes, again."

Vova, confused, but compliant, picked up a stone and threw it at Sadavir.

A collective gasp erupted from the watching crowd as a pile of scrap metal no one had noticed at Sadavir's feet shaped itself instantly into a shield that covered Sadavir. The thrown rock bounced harmlessly off the hard shell. The blue light that shown out of Aric's fist faded and he handed both Stones to Andre, who then held his hand out to Sadavir. The shield shrunk and fell away. The next time Sadavir spoke, there wasn't another sound in all of the camp.

"The Stones were meant to work together." He proclaimed. "If we work together, we don't need to kill them to stop them, and we certainly don't need to be killed."

Suddenly, the two masses, Creators and Destroyers, meshed, each person searching for someone who had a match for their own Stone. In some areas, stones were already being shaped into strange designs. From the far side of the meadow, a green light grew in the hand of one of the Destroyers as trees and brush were removed out of his path. Ivan shouted excitedly to Sadavir.

"We can make the wall unbreachable, Sadavir, we don't have to fight them!"

Sadavir reclaimed the attention of the crowd.

"We must face them! Don't you understand? This wall should never have been built in the first place. We should not be two separate peoples. We must face this army and defeat it. And we must defeat it without killing anybody."

He paused to let the effects of his words ripple through the crowd.

"Our fears and our hate will be the undoing of both our peoples. We were meant to work together, that is the true purpose of the Stones. It has always been the ultimate destiny of our people. And we must begin today."

A few of the people, mostly the older ones in the crowd, were already nodding, but others, including Vova, still looked troubled.

"Sadavir, if you order us to stand against this army and not kill them, I will follow you." Vova spoke loud enough for everyone to hear. "But I do not understand why we should risk our lives and the future of our people to preserve these invaders. They are the ones who have attacked, don't we have the right to defend ourselves?"

All eyes had turned back to Sadavir, awaiting his reply. I took a moment to reflect on the odd scene that lay before me. Sadavir was only barely over twenty years of age. Vova was his senior by many years. Glancing around the crowd, I guessed that, discounting the children, Sadavir was the youngest in the crowd, and yet all looked to him.

There was a quality that was sometimes found in certain men. Those who studied such things called it charisma. I have always believed it to be something deeper. Certainly, charisma did not apply to this youth with tousled hair that stood nervous in front of staring eyes. But men could feel his courage, they trusted in his wisdom even before he spoke. Sadavir did not wish to be a leader; he hadn't sought it. At that moment, he was certainly wishing that he could have been anywhere else in the world. But as hard as the task might be, no matter what it took from him, he

195

could not back down if the victims of his cowardice would be truth and right.

Action in fear, integrity in despair. Such is greatness.

"What will happen if we do kill them?" Sadavir spoke softly, but his voice was heard clearly by all. He didn't wait, but answered his own question.

"We will make more bitterness on their side. How long before new weapons are created? How long before they come up with new ways of killing us or sealing us out of their world?

"I've seen how you live here. If the weather is hard, will your wives be cold? If there is drought, will your children go hungry?

"You are the ones attacked, it is true, and you have every right to defend yourselves and your families. But even in their deaths they will defeat you. For their widows will cry themselves to sleep in stone houses out of the weather. Their children will grow up fatherless in streets among neighbors who have the means to share.

"You have the right to kill them, it is true. But will you? Knowing what it would mean to your families, will you? Vova?"

Sadavir directed his question directly at Vova, a daring stroke. Vova's heart held more bitterness than almost all of the others, his would be, by far, the most convincing testimony, one way or the other. Vova knew it too and paused to think before he answered.

"No, Sadavir, I will not. I don't know if the Creators will ever share their world with us. But if my death would even buy us a chance, I give it freely."

Sadavir continued Vova's line of thought. "Victory could be

gained cheaply enough. But I offer all of us a chance to start a new age. A brand new era where none are slaves, none are outcasts, and there's enough to go around for everyone."

The rest of the crowd offered no further objections. It was Faisal, one of the Creators, who voiced the next question.

"So how will we defeat them without killing them? They do have a lot of weapons."

Sadavir's expression spoke of his relief as he passed the attention away from himself.

"Actually, Andre has a plan, and I'll let him explain it to you."

Sadavir gratefully melted into the crowd as they all huddled around Andre, who was already drawing in the dirt. I smiled as the plan unfolded.

I liked Andre.

Chapter 24

The calm before a storm should mean nothing. It is literally nothing, but it somehow has the power to pull the deepest thoughts and emotions from the human heart.
　　　　　　　　　　　　　–Musings of the Historian

I lay on my back watching the stars above me. It was a moonless night and the stars lit the night sky, burning in their own silent infernos. I heard a rustle in the grass next to me. It was Sadavir.

"So, Sadavir, can't you sleep?" I asked as he sat down next to me.

He shook his head and smiled.

"Walking over here I passed seven other men. I have yet to see anyone sleeping tonight." Sadavir fell silent for a moment before he spoke his next question.

"Uncle, have you seen war before?"

I nodded, my eyes still on the stars.

"I'm afraid." He admitted openly. I turned my head to look at him.

"You've already seen a fair bit of battle yourself, Sadavir, surely you've gotten used to it a bit. Dealing with larger numbers actually isn't all that different than dealing with small numbers. It's all about position."

"It's not that, Uncle. I have my armbands, and I have my

Stone. And this is what my life is supposed to mean. I do not fear for myself, but what of my father? What of my mother? What of…" His voice trailed off and I heard the name he never spoke. He resumed without finishing his last sentence.

"How will I be able to protect them? They have no black Stone; they have no armbands. How will I be able to concentrate on what I have to do when I'm looking around to see if they're all right? What if I fail them? What if they die?"

"Sadavir," I began, choosing my words carefully. "You might fail them."

His eyes raised to the stars. Even in the dark I could see the tears form in the corners of his eyes. I continued.

"But there have been a thousand times I have seen you where you might have failed them. You haven't let them down yet. They are very proud of what you've become.

"The possibility of failure is very real. It haunts all thinking beings. You will always live with that fear, everyone does. But will that fear stop you from trying?

"When we were in that dungeon under Saddhan's house, you depended on Aric to dig you out and Olya to heal you. What if they had failed you?"

"But they wouldn't have, Uncle." Sadavir's voice was insistent.

"Why not? They are human, they could have failed."

"I don't know why, they just wouldn't have failed, they would have made sure it worked out some way or another, I just know it."

"How do you know it?" I pressed.

"I don't know." He reiterated.

"Yes, Sadavir, you do. You just aren't saying it. The answer is right in front of you."

He thought for a moment, and then smiled, his arms dropping to his armbands.

"Was that a joke, Uncle? I don't think I've ever heard you tell a joke. I see what you're saying, though. You're saying that they wouldn't have failed me because they love me?"

I nodded, barely visible in the darkness.

"So are you saying that I won't fail them because I love them?"

"The answer is right in front of you, Sadavir." I repeated. "You won't let yourself fail."

"Thanks, Uncle. How did you become so wise?" he asked with almost childlike curiosity.

"Because I'm old, boy, now go to bed."

"Sure, maybe I can sleep a little." Sadavir said and slipped noiselessly back into the night. I waited a moment after he left, studying the stars.

"You can come out now, Olya." I spoke into the night. I was answered by more footsteps, these much quieter.

"I didn't want to interrupt you. I didn't know you saw me." Olya whispered as she lowered herself down to the ground in the very spot Sadavir had sat only a moment before.

"I heard a twig snap in the bushes as Sadavir was getting up to leave. The only other person who would be coming to talk to me is Aric, and that man moves about as quietly as a falling tree."

"Well, you certainly seem to be in high spirits, Uncle. Doesn't it bother you that men might die tomorrow, or even tonight, if they get through the gate?"

"Well, I don't think that they will try a night attack, their advantage depends on good lighting.

"As for my feelings, I am no more anxious to see anyone die than you are. But the deaths of men aren't what interest me, it's their lives. And tomorrow will be a defining moment for thousands of lives, both present and future, whatever the outcome may be."

"You are a strange one, Uncle."

I smiled in the darkness.

"I've been hearing that a lot lately." I responded.

"What do you think of Andre's plan, Uncle?"

"I think it shows a great deal of cunning. I don't think anyone but Andre could have realized the potential of the Stones faster than Andre did."

"I don't like it." Olya blurted out.

I raised an eyebrow.

"And what is it you don't like about the plan, Olya?"

"Don't you think it depends too much on one man?"

"You mean Sadavir?" I asked.

"Yes," Olya said, exasperated. "What happens if something happens to him, the whole plan would fail."

"So you're afraid of what will happen if the plan fails? Worried for your people?" I turned away so that she wouldn't see my smile.

"Well, no." She admitted. "I mean yes! I mean, of course I'm worried about my people, I've seen what those weapons can do. It's just that..." Her voice trailed off.

"Don't worry, Olya, even if Sadavir gets killed, we'll figure out some way of stopping them."

"I know, I know, but I don't want…" She stopped as her voice started to crack.

"You don't want Sadavir to die." I finished for her, rolling back over to face her.

She nodded, not trusting her voice.

"I understand, little one. And you should know that he loves you too. As for your fears, I only have one piece of advice. There is a very small voice inside you that tells you that the sun rises in Sadavir's eyes, and that he can do anything. All women in love hear that voice. It's not reason, it's not even true, but you need to listen to that voice tonight."

"Thanks, Uncle. I'll try." Olya said, standing. I smiled at the stars; they seemed to laugh with me.

"You should get some sleep too." I said out loud once Olya was out of hearing range.

"Silent as a falling tree, eh? I should kick you where you lay, you conniver, it would serve you right."

Aric's large shadowy form separated itself from a large stone and he walked away. He only paused once.

"Will it all be all right, Amar? You seem to know something we don't." Aric's voice was low, but it carried well in the still night air.

"All I can promise is that the sun will rise tomorrow. And that is enough."

Aric chuckled softly.

"More than twenty years you have lived and worked with my family, Amar. I don't think I've got a straight answer from you yet."

"Maybe you just didn't ask the right questions, Aric."

I could see his head shake.

"Good night, Amar."

Good night, Aric.

Chapter 25

A thing doesn't have to be threatening for people to fear it, it only has to be unexpected.
        –Musings of the Historian

In the morning, the birds' songs were interrupted by a loud crashing coming from the gate. Saddhan had abandoned finesse and seemed intent now on simply knocking the door from its hinges. On my side of the gate, preparations were finishing. I liked the look of things, this would be a unique battle.

Following Andre's orders, I climbed a tree and hid myself, content in my role as an observer in the coming fray.

Sadavir had blocked the door by jamming stones and large pieces of wood against the door. It was a quickly done job, but it had been effective. The heavy doors needed a lot of force just to swing them anyway; any sort of obstruction would make it that much worse.

Saddhan's army would have been far better served by long, steady pressure that would have slowly shifted the door open, but Saddhan's rage had closed his mind to options. The bloodlust flowed through his mind like lava, burning his reason and leaving only the black ash of hate and lust for power.

The workmanship of the door held well against the attacks from the army, but after a while, the stone in which the hinges were lodged started to crack. It wasn't long until the doors reluctantly released their hold on the wall and fell forward into the Destroyers' land. The army immediately flooded in, ready for anything. As they ran in, they spread out and searched the landscape for some sort of resistance, aching for an enemy. The landscape was empty, they were greeted only by trampled grass and trees swaying lightly in the breeze.

Saddhan came through near the middle of the army. His eyes swept the landscape, lingering the longest on a large tree that grew near the gate. He stared at it suspiciously, searching its branches. He seemed disturbed by its very presence, as if it were something that didn't belong. Finally shaking his head, he walked on, already shouting orders to those on the Destroyers' side of the wall as the rest of the army filed in.

As the last of the army came in, Saddhan placed himself in front of them all.

"Now, you have all followed me in here to do a job that's needed doing for a very long time, for as long as we can all remember. Follow me now and we will finish it. Now, give these animals no mercy, for you certainly will receive none from them. Beware when they act afraid, they are probably planning some sort..." Saddhan's voice trailed off as his eyes locked on the gate behind the army.

"...not possible... GET TO THE GATE!" He screamed. The army acted as one as they spun around to look at the gate, which seemed to have melted, although it gave off no heat. The metal flowed upward, filling the space it had vacated only minutes before. The metal solidified, making a new gate. But this one was without hinges, without bars, it simply locked into the rock, forming a solid metal patch on the wounded wall. All their attention was locked on the wall. None noticed the faint blue light that emitted from a hole in the large tree. The men with the green stones had done their work perfectly, no part of the tree betrayed the fact that it held two men within. I smiled. It was a beautiful, warm day. Aric would already be regretting his part in this battle.

The men threw themselves against it, trying to get their fingers around an edge to pull the new gate off of the wall, all to no avail. All coming to the same conclusion at once, they turned their backs to the gate, raising their weapons, waiting for an attack. The silent moments dragged on as they were answered only by a gentle breeze that wandered its way across the field.

It was a unique tactic. I wasn't aware of another battle where the commanding general had chosen to seal an invading army inside his own territory.

The men grew restless and already a few questioning whispers spoke the thoughts of the group.

"Where are they?"

"Why don't they attack?"

Finally, one man among them realized that there was a far more troubling question that needed answering.

"Why would they do that?" He said, already louder than a whisper. Standing from where he had been kneeling and lowering his weapon, he asked louder.

"Why would they want to keep us from returning to our own land?"

Just watching the faces of the men, I could see the waves of panic wash over the army as they realized the true implications of what they had just seen. The same man who had asked the question also spoke their fears.

"They could be attacking our families. We've left them defenseless."

Several men were looking sick with worry. Several weapons dropped to the ground, followed by the men who carried them as they sunk to their knees, burying their heads in their hands.

"We have to keep going!" Saddhan yelled at the men, desperately trying to maintain control. "We need to finish the job we came here to do. We must be strong!"

"Why?" The man's tone was low, but his voice trembled with emotion. He continued, louder. "Why should we continue on? To ensure that our families will be safe in the future? They're not safe now!" Veins bulged out of the man's neck as he screamed at Saddhan.

"We can't turn back now!" Saddhan insisted. "You have to listen to me."

"No! No, Saddhan, I will not listen. I have listened to you so far and now my family could already be dead! You are the one who brought us here. It was your hatred that brought us to this. If my family is harmed, Saddhan… I blame you!"

The man had started to walk slowly toward Saddhan. Saddhan, suddenly realizing how sharply the tides had changed, raised his weapon defensively to point at the man. Several of the weapons in the army raised to point at Saddhan. Saddhan noticed the weapons and tried desperately to reclaim his hold on the people.

"We can still save your families!" He yelled. The man who was approaching him paused.

"We're listening, Saddhan, but you had better talk fast."

"We still have the axes we brought with us to chop down

the tree we used for a battering ram. We can chop down other trees and prop them up against the walls. That will get us over the spikes. Then we can simply drop down on the other side. It's quite a drop, but we could make it."

Saddhan had grasped at straws, but it had paid off. The men looked around for the axes. Only handles were found. The axes had been dropped on the ground next to the gate as they had rushed through, thinking only of their weapons. I had no doubt that the metal from the axe heads now helped form the very barrier the men were trying to breach.

"Any more bright ideas, Saddhan?" The man turned on Saddhan once more, his worry for his family translating into anger at Saddhan.

Saddhan again raised his weapon to point at the man's chest. He had run out of ideas, but even in defeat, he would lash out. He yelped as the launcher in his hand suddenly fell apart. He jumped back from the pieces, staring at them. Several of the men displayed the same reaction as their weapons also dismantled in their hands. It was only a matter of time before the milling army was left with only metal components littering the ground at their feet.

"What kind of trickery is this?" Saddhan wondered out loud as he stared at the spectacle.

"It's actually not all that hard." Sadavir announced as he walked casually toward the army. During the destruction of the weapons, no one had noticed as he had dropped soundlessly from his tree and started his stroll toward the confused army.

"Get him! It's the traitor, he's the one to blame, kill him!" Saddhan raged. No one was listening to him now. They merely stared at Sadavir as if he were a specter from beyond the grave.

Only Padam, blinded by rage, rushed at Sadavir. He ran at him and grabbed at Sadavir, aiming to tackle him to ground. His arms flailed as they hit empty air. Sadavir had dropped to the side, leaving only his extended leg behind where he had stood only a moment before. Padam tripped and hit the ground hard. His hand found a fallen limb and he jumped from the ground, swinging the thick branch like a club. Sadavir easily dodged his first two swings. Padam then tried to jab with the branch, thrusting with it like a sword. Sadavir sidestepped and caught hold of the branch, jerking it away from his attacker.

Padam started to scramble back toward the army, but suddenly spun back to Sadavir, throwing a handful of sand toward his eyes. Sadavir, expecting a rock, had flashed his armband forward through the path of the thrown dirt, but failed to block the mass of dirt. He sprung back as the dirt filled his eyes.

Padam took full advantage of his small victory and leapt in, kicking Sadavir hard in the stomach. The wind flew out of Sadavir as if from his father's blacksmith bellows and he fell backwards.

Padam was on top of him in a moment, punching and scratching. Saddhan, for his part, was screaming at the army for them to help his son. The army seemed confused at the new turn of events and paid no heed to Saddhan's screeches, content to watch idly as the events played out in front of them.

Padam had made a mistake by jumping on top of Sadavir.

Although still blinded, Sadavir's armored forearms flew in front of his chest, trying to defend himself. His armband slammed into Padam's fist as it passed and Padam rolled off to the side, gasping and holding his injured hand.

"Look out!" Olya's voice was unmistakable as she screamed

a warning. Several eyes flashed to the tree that she was hiding in, but flashed back to see the thing that she had warned Sadavir about.

As Sadavir rose to his feet, still trying to blink the sand out of his eyes, Saddhan had abandoned his attempts of persuading the army and had picked up the club that Sadavir had dropped and now crept silently up behind the blinded Sadavir. My breath caught in my throat as Saddhan swung hard for Sadavir's head.

The club broke in half as Sadavir's armband met the club mid-swing. Even from my high vantage point, I could see his black Stone shimmer and dance violently on his chest. Sadavir's closed eyes stared in front of him and I was reminded of the day behind his father's house and the pile of broken wooden balls. Saddhan stumbled back, his hands and wrists shocked by the impact.

Sadavir finally managed to open one eye and peered through it at Saddhan.

"Please don't kill me, Sadavir." Saddhan had gone from treacherous warrior to pleading beggar in the blink of an eye. He fell to his knees as he pleaded for his life. Sadavir waved him back to the army. Saddhan scampered back into the ranks of the army, followed closely by his son.

Sadavir approached the waiting army again, staring at them through bloodshot eyes. Several of the men looked around for weapons, but most just waited, not knowing what to expect.

"Creators! You have invaded our land!" Sadavir announced. "We have destroyed your weapons, you are at our mercy!"

"I only see one of you, boy!" The man who had confronted Saddhan now confronted Sadavir. He was from a different village and had never met Sadavir. Men from Sadavir's village hissed warnings at the man, but went unheeded.

"It would only take me to scatter your army." Sadavir responded threateningly. The man scoffed.

"You are only a boy, what gives you the idea you could defeat us all?"

With bloodshot eyes and a dirty face, Sadavir still held an air of majesty as he addressed the army.

"I could defeat you because you are cowards!" Sadavir's opening remark rippled through the ranks of the army, the men stirring angrily at his words.

"I could defeat you because you haven't the spine to stand up to one hateful man and his lust for power. I could defeat you because you are fat, gorged on your unshared wealth. I could defeat you because you are blind, blind to the suffering that happens every day beyond your walls.

"I could defeat you because I have honor." Sadavir pulled his black Stone from around his head.

"I could defeat you because I have love." He pulled a small, clear Stone from the pouch that hung at his side.

Putting both the Stones in one hand, he raised it for everyone to see as the black light jumped and danced between the Stones and down over his arms. The army drew back in fear and wonder. Sadavir thrust his hand to the side of the army and a section of the wall burst outward in a thunder crack of pure destruction.

"Now go home!" Sadavir ordered the cowering army. "Your families are safe. Far safer than ours were at your mercy."

The man who had been acting as spokesman for the army

stared at the gaping hole in the wall.

"Do all Destroyers have this power? Is that how they got over the wall?" The man wondered out loud.

"The Destroyers never went over the wall." Sadavir announced. Several of the men, who had already started to head toward the hole in the wall, turned to protest. Sadavir interrupted them.

"They went right through that gate and it was opened by one of your own." He declared.

"Who would do such a thing?" The man demanded.

"I ask you, good sir, who stands to gain when people are driven by fear? Who profits when the people will sacrifice their freedom for safety?" Sadavir paused and smiled. "Who is a jerk with a really annoying voice?"

I knew that Sadavir was taking a chance. He didn't really know who had been opening the door, all he had to go on was a very vague description given him by Andre. His gamble paid off, however, as Saddhan groveled and begged for his life.

"No, it's a misunderstanding! I never meant to... if you kill me it would be murder... murder! I have a wife and a son, they need a husband and father..." His voice trailed off into whimpering as the man who had been speaking looked on in disgust. He turned back to Sadavir.

"We will leave your lands, but we will make more of the weapons, we will be ready to defend ourselves." The man warned. Sadavir smiled, his eyes looking meaningfully to the gaping hole in the wall.

"Defend yourselves, eh?"

The man was left with no response and merely turned his

212

back on Sadavir and followed the army as they crossed through the wall back to their own land.

As soon as the last of them had gone through, a few more people dropped out of the trees. Two men with green stones approached the tree that grew next to the gate. The Creator gave his Stone to the other man, who held his hand up to the tree.

The tree twitched and shimmered as it shrunk and twisted itself back into the ground that had given it birth. As the trunk twisted away, it revealed a hollow chamber in its very middle. Aric burst out as soon as there was a space big enough, gasping for air. Andre followed after with his customary amused smile still fixed on his face.

"Come then, Aric, it wasn't all that bad, was it?" Andre asked. Aric only glared at him in response. Andre laughed, then turned to Sadavir, who was trying to convince Olya that he truly was all right and that his eyes didn't need to be healed.

"So, Sadavir, part one went well." Andre started. Sadavir nodded, a small smile of relief growing on his face. Andre continued.

"Now it's our turn to invade."

Sadavir nodded somberly. Then, his mood suddenly lightening, he turned to Olya.

"Would you mind taking a walk with me?"

I watched, amused, as Sadavir started walking down the length of the wall. Periodically, his arm would raise and another section of the hated wall would burst and crumble to the ground. Spontaneous cheers erupted from the watching crowd with each thunder blast of broken rock and swirling dust.

Chapter 26

Fear spreads, this explains many of man's worst moments, but so does faith, and that explains man's redemption.

–Musings of the Historian

The next day, a considerable army of Destroyers stood staring at the rubble that remained from the wall. Intermingled with the Destroyers were the several Creators who had followed Aric. They had long since given up their uneasiness about being around those whom they had feared for so long and now enthusiastically assisted Andre in showing the new recruits what the Stones were capable of when they were placed together.

As I watched the numbers in the army grow, I grew concerned about the intentions of the army. Good intentions were soon misguided when they were confronted with large numbers of supporters. It wasn't long before the first voice of bitterness voiced itself above the mumbling of the others. It sounded a lot like Vova's first protest, but this time it was backed by over a hundred others who seemed to also think it was a good idea.

"Now that the wall is down, why don't we just take what we need from the Creators?" A nameless Destroyer yelled out. "They've starved us out for as long as any one of us can remember. I think it's about time they felt what it was like!"

Several people yelled in support.

"Don't you people understand?" Surprisingly, it was Vova

who first answered the angry cry. "War will only bring more war, we have to do this peacefully!"

The crowd, however, had drawn courage from its numbers and the spokesman wouldn't be convinced so easily.

"Have these Creators robbed you of your courage, Vova? I remember the day well when you vowed to kill every Creator you ever saw to avenge the death of your father. Have you forgotten him so easily?" Vova cringed under the assault, the words cutting him deeply. Sadavir intervened.

"If any of you wish to exact your revenge on the Creators, you are free to do so." He announced. The head of every Creator in the camp snapped up to look at Sadavir. Sadavir was not finished, however.

"But you must first know that I am a sworn protector of the Creators. I will not allow you to hurt them as long as I am alive."

"The Stone around your neck is that of a Destroyer." The man protested. "Would you betray your own people?"

"It is because you are my people that I broke down the wall." Sadavir answered. "But the Creators are also my people, I will not betray them either. So if you want blood, you must start with mine."

"Will you give Olya back her Stone? Or will you simply wipe us out if we try anything against you?"

Sadavir smiled, handing the clear Stone to Olya. "I claim no advantage over you. You are free to try whatever you would like."

"Come on then!" The man yelled. "Whoever would be true to their families and their dead loved ones, let's remove this traitor from our eyes!" Several of the newcomers separated themselves from the crowd and formed together into a crowd of about fifteen and they slowly advanced on Sadavir.

"People are dumb." Aric concluded as he stood next to me. I grinned.

The crowd instinctively spread out to encircle Sadavir. But this time, Sadavir did not wait for them to attack. Running straight at the man who had been the spokesman, Sadavir jumped straight into the air, landing with his knee on the man's shoulders and slamming his elbow down hard on the man's head. The man went down hard before any of his fellows could even react. Sadavir rolled and stood to face the rest of them. They continued to circle, more wary this time.

"This is war!" Sadavir yelled as he pounced on another, sweeping his legs out from under him and slamming a fist into the man's face before he had even landed. Before the others could converge on him, he was gone again, leaving the man unconscious on the ground.

"This is what awaits you if you persist." Sadavir again sprang, this time catching two by their necks, ducking easily under their blows. He pushed them back hard and both flew to their backs. An almost unseen movement from Sadavir's hands and these two were lying peacefully on the ground. The others grabbed him from behind but Sadavir kicked his legs up over the back of the person holding him and the man was thrown backwards to the ground as Sadavir again twisted away like a shadow.

"How long before your wives are widows, before your children are orphans?" Trying a new strategy, the remaining ten rushed him all at once. Leaping straight into the air, Sadavir leapfrogged over their charge and landed on the far side of the rushing crowd, kicking backwards at the men as they tried to switch directions. Several toppled from the unexpected move. They staggered up from the dust. They no longer seemed certain of their cause.

"Does it matter who attacks or who defends? Everyone is hurt!" This time there was no charge from either side, the men started to look very uneasy, obviously wishing now that they had stayed among the army. More than just losing, they looked ridiculous.

"Does anyone else want war?" Sadavir had turned toward the army. "If you do, come out now and get your fill. As for me, I had more than I ever wanted after my first fight. Anyone?"

"ANYONE?!" He yelled again, his face red. The silence was ominous as no one even dared move.

"Take your Stones in your hands." Sadavir commanded. The heat of the moment had given his voice great authority. There was a flurry of confused motion as every man, woman, and child reached into pouches, pockets, and necklaces as they complied with his order.

"Now swear by your Stones that you will make no more war, and that you will obey my commands, mine and Andre's." There was a low din as everyone responded in their own way. But everyone responded. One brave man raised his voice.

"Do you also so swear, Sadavir?" It was one of the Creators from Sadavir's village. The fear that had first driven Sadavir from his home was not easily forgotten.

"Not yet." Sadavir admitted. "There might still be need for war yet, but I will be the army. That is what I was made for. Anyone else with a black Stone may join me." The bitterness was evident in his voice.

I had no doubt of Sadavir's fighting ability, that had been proven many times over, but now I began to wonder if this war would be won at the cost of Sadavir's soul. The bitterness was welling up in his soul and as he lashed out with it, he was obeyed. His growing anger was being reinforced by the people who fed off it and respected him for it. Although determined not to intervene, I secretly prayed that the ordeal would end soon. In truth, no matter how strong the boy was, the strain was too much to ask of someone so young.

His tactics were working, however, the people had found a leader. He had won them over with his skill, his words, and his passion. They would obey him without question now. I had seen it before. It had seldom ended well.

I was relieved when it was Andre who moved to take control of the army. He gave orders and organized men and support as if he had been a general for his whole life.

More grass was trampled into dust, but eventually the army was underway, stepping almost gleefully over the rubble that represented what was left of the barrier that had mocked them for almost their whole lives. Still, they were more than careful to avoid the black-tipped wooden spikes that lay among the debris.

I smiled at some of the children who jumped up and down on come of the larger bricks as if to pound them deeper into the ground.

The army had not walked far before it met resistance. Several men from a local village gathered together to face the approaching army. They looked scared to death as they faced the approaching army, grasping farm implements in their white-knuckled hands. No doubt all of them would have run if they

218

could, but their families were at their backs. I suspected that the men's bravery was a diversion to cover their family's flight.

Black light rippled in Sadavir's fist and the ground in between the men and the approaching army exploded. The awesome power of the Stones broke the last of the men's spirits as they were showered by dust and small rock fragments. They threw down their weapons and fell to their knees, hoping against hope for mercy.

My concern for Sadavir grew as I now saw him resorting immediately to the violent force of the two Stones. I wondered if Olya would help pull him back, but she followed him with absolute loyalty. In her eyes, nothing Sadavir could do would ever be wrong.

The looks of shock on the villagers' faces were evident as they were lifted from the ground by friendly hands. Smiling faces introduced themselves while helping hands dusted the men off and handed them water from leather sacks. The men walked as if in a dream, not believing what was happening. The army came upon the village that the men were guarding.

The village had been built when the wall had first come into being as a camp for the workers. The people quivering in front of us now were their descendants. Such a sight as the one that lay before them had not been seen in ages. All who had not fled now stood hopelessly, waiting and watching to see their homes destroyed.

The army descended upon the village like locusts. The crowds of men and even women moving through the village were met by screams as people ran from them.

When the horde reorganized on the far side of the village, however, the screams had turned into an awed silence as the people stared at what had been done.

Stumps that had marred the farmland were suddenly gone. Broken down houses were repaired, the workmanship surpassing even the finest of the Creator masters. Even the fruit trees now lay heavy with fruit, the branches holding the load strong and thick.

The army looked back on its workmanship with pride. In just under fifteen minutes, the run down hamlet had been turned into a thriving, beautiful village, the houses finer than the richest houses of the largest villages. The army turned and walked on, saying nothing.

No one explained, no invitations were extended, but several of the villagers ran to join up with the moving army. They were greeted warmly by the invaders who were still exhilarated by their stunning "victory." The energy of the people was vibrant and caught on quickly. People had no idea what was happening, but it felt good. They would think about it later.

At the next village, they met with more resistance as the people who had run from the first village had warned the next village of the coming danger, not knowing of the final outcome. Expecting as much, Sadavir walked far in front of the army. The token resistance presented itself, standing in a tight group. The real attack came from the trees as men tried to kill Sadavir, hoping to demoralize the army with the death of its leader.

When the stones that were thrown proved ineffective, the men charged, en masse, at Sadavir. It wasn't long before they were all gasping for breath, unharmed and unarmed. The army folded around the defenders and they were swept up in bewilderment as they were greeted by members of the other village who explained what had happened at the last village.

This time, several of the members of the last village gave

their Stones and their support to the cause as they helped sweep through the village. The imperfect and the flawed was fixed, the unfixable ceased to exist altogether. The army again paused at the far edge of town to survey their handiwork. The effect was the same. Destroyers and Creators laughed and boasted their feats together, giddy and lost in their new world. Not understanding, not asking to.

As they neared Sadavir's village, the resistance became more intense. Already several launchers were being used against Sadavir. The men were disarmed quickly, cowed, and picked up by the rag-tag army, which had now swelled in size to almost four hundred, not counting the many children who tried to run behind the army as it moved triumphantly through the land.

Sadavir was tireless as he fought band after band of defenders. A hard determination burned in his eyes, but the light mood of the army was getting to him as well. I caught a smile flick across his lips as he watched Olya dancing with one of the Creator children.

As we drew closer to Sadavir's village, however, the mood darkened. Several in the army had marched with Saddhan. They knew well of his hatred and his guile. All were on their guard.

As they walked by a forest not too far from Sadavir's village, the unmistakable sound of a released launcher was heard from the trees. A black form slid back into the woods. Sadavir spun around, the rock had not been launched at him. It wasn't hard to find the victim. A man held his side with both hands as a dark stain spread through his shirt, his teeth clenched against the pain.

"Papa! For Olya!" Sadavir yelled back at the army and threw his black Stone at his father as he turned and ran toward the forest. Aric caught the stone deftly and tossed it gently to Olya, who ran to the man who was now seated on the ground. Sadavir must have had his mind on the man as he ran into the forest after the sniper, because the stones in Olya's hand glowed and a look of relief grew on the man's face.

The army didn't have to wait long before Sadavir reemerged from the forest, shaking his head. He had not found the would-be assassin. On rejoining the army, Sadavir called for everyone who had a light blue stone to come forward. Again, his orders were obeyed immediately as people ran to the front. Sadavir instructed the Creators with light blue stones to give their stones to a Destroyer and to join them in walking on the outside of the army, warning them to be diligent in searching the woods for any sort of motion at all, entrusting the safety of the army to the reflexes of the Destroyers.

It wasn't long before another attempt was made. Stones launched out of the woods. This time, hands glowing with pale blue light raised and the projectiles disintegrated into dust mid-air. Again, Sadavir rushed into the forest after them. This time, there were sounds of an intense struggle. The moments dragged on as the army held its collective breath. They gasped as Sadavir burst from the trees, dragging someone behind him, blood running down his leg and from a deep gouge on his face. He paused to whip his arm behind him, blocking another stone launched at him.

Several of the army surged forward to assist him, but he waved them back. When he reached the army, Olya has immediately pulling the Stone from his neck and holding both Stones, glowing, over his wounds. Aric grabbed the person that Sadavir had pulled in. It was Padam; he was unconscious.

"It was a trap." Sadavir explained. "I chased Padam into a

clearing and six launchers fired at me at the exact same time. I blocked two and dodged two, but one got me in the leg and the other gave me this scratch on my face."

Olya didn't even respond as she held the Stones over his face as the wounds closed. Everyone around was thinking the same thing. Another inch to the side and the stone would have taken his life. His aura of immortality had taken a hit. His army had seen him bleed. The mood in the army suddenly became more subdued, almost melancholy.

Any children in the party were immediately pulled into the middle of the army, all the men now searched the tree line for any sign of the unseen enemies. Padam was trussed up and carried,like a sack of flour.

There was only one more stand of trees left between them and the village that was thick enough to conceal an attack and the entire army felt the surge of fear and adrenaline that comes from expecting an attack.

This time, against Olya and Aric's protests, Sadavir took the offensive, marching toward the trees ahead of the army. A shot was fired and shattered against Sadavir's armband. Cursing came from the trees as Sadavir broke into a run towards where the shot had come from.

Rather than running into the trees as before, however, as Sadavir reached the trees, he sprang into the branches of the nearest tree. Surprised shouts came from the trees as Sadavir crept, like a spider, through the trees. This time, there was no sound of general struggle, only a lone startled scream and then silence, then another.

After a few minutes, Sadavir reappeared outside the trees and waved the army in. They picked up several more unconscious men. Padam, in the meantime, had regained consciousness and was now cursing loudly.

"Swine! Wretched peasants! Cowards!" The army endured his vehemence for only about a minute, when they realized that he wasn't stopping. A small piece of wood was placed inside his mouth and suddenly expanded under the glowing green light of the Stones. The makeshift gag was too big for him to get past his teeth, but it did not interfere with his breathing. After that, all they heard from Padam was high-pitched, gurgling wails as he tried to scream around the wooden mass in his mouth.

Sadavir commanded the army to stop and rest as he called Andre and Aric to him. I wasn't invited, but came anyway.

"Saddhan wasn't among the ones captured in the forest." Sadavir observed. "I'm guessing that he's gone ahead to the village. I also haven't seen very many of the men from the army that he led through the gate. The invasion may have been enough for him to regain some control. If he has, our entry into that village isn't going to be pleasant at all."

Andre nodded.

"He has a good line of vision coming from that village, he will be able to see us coming, we won't get close enough to dismantle his weapons with the Stones before he is firing on us. There will be too many launchers to dodge or block." Andre stated.

"And knowing him he will have all of his soldiers shoot first and ask questions later, so we won't be able to get close enough to talk to them." Aric added.

"Saddhan will have them thinking that this is their last chance, I don't think they'll run. A direct attack won't work... not if we don't want to get someone killed." Sadavir concluded.

"Perhaps some will die then, Sadavir." Andre said, no stranger to the cruelties of life. I was surprised when Sadavir nodded.

"That may be so, and if it comes to that, we still must not fail. But I will not consider that option until it is our last resort." Sadavir insisted.

"Ok then," Andre said, suddenly cheering. "If they are expecting a mighty battle, we must not disappoint them."

"What are you talking about, Andre?" Aric asked.

"I'm talking about giving them the battle they want. Their main advantage is that they are the defenders. They can ambush, they can hide behind walls and fire at us with us barely being able to see them. So we have to draw them out, or find a way of getting in close."

"From your tone, I'm guessing that you already have a plan."

Andre smiled.

We'll wait till nightfall. In the meantime, make a big show of setting up camp. Make sure the women are near the front in setting things up, I'm betting that a lot of those men have wives in our army. Let them start to doubt.

Chapter 27

Man is slow because he hesitates.

–Musings of the Historian

As the light started to fail, Saddhan responded by creating a perimeter of bonfires around the town, maintaining his line of vision to protect against a surprise attack in the night. The men tending the fires always held burning torches.

"Now why do you figure they're holding torches when the fires are burning high right next to them?" Aric wondered out loud.

"This Saddhan is a smart one." Andre smiled. "If we take out one of those guards, his torch will fall to the ground and Saddhan will know that we're trying something. No doubt he has at least one man for every torch, just watching."

"So then what do we do?" Sadavir wondered out loud.

"We give him exactly what he's waiting for." Andre responded.

Andre only smiled in response to Sadavir's and Aric's quizzical looks. He turned to rejoin the army as Sadavir and Aric hurried to keep up with him.

"I only have one question, Sadavir." Andre began. "When you use those Stones together, how wide of a column of destruction does it make, can you focus it?"

Sadavir nodded. "It's not really even a column or beam at

all, the Stones merely destroy what I'm focusing on, whether it's a huge stone wall or a tiny blade of grass."

"Perfect, then you will be our first line of attack." Andre said, pleased.

"And, uh… what is it that I am attacking?" Sadavir asked.

"My warrior friend," Andre stopped and laid his hand on Sadavir's shoulder in mock gravity. "Tonight you will do battle with fires, and slay many."

Sadavir just shook his head as Andre turned again and continued marching on to the army. Finally standing in front of the army, he addressed them.

"I need about a hundred men who can move very quietly and can take a man down without killing him. I need warriors." The last sentence was added in almost as an afterthought, but his meaning was made clear. All of the men who stepped forward wore Destroyers' Stones and walked with cat-like agility. The Creators were willing enough, but their experience had only taught them to walk in plowed fields and packed-dirt streets, they knew nothing of the stealth needed to live in the wilds.

Andre looked pleased at the selection. He obviously knew many of the men who now faced him.

Beckoning them closer, he explained his plan. Then, sending them off to find their positions, he turned to the rest of the waiting army and explained their duty to them. As for me, I walked a fair bit off to the side into the night, where I could see everything that would go in, both with the army and in the village.

The last of the light left the sky, the stars shining brightly. It was indeed a good night for such an attack; there was no moon out that night. Only the bonfires cut swathes of light into the blackness of the night.

Suddenly, one of the fires closest to the army exploded into the night. The fire was instantly extinguished as the logs and coals that fed it were scattered into the air in the blink of an eyelid. The coals were spread out far and wide, some men cursed and jumped as some of the coals found their ways onto shirts and trousers. The coals pulsed red with light with the passing of the night breeze, a red glowing mirror of the night sky above them.

Shouts of alarm were raised from the village. The men who had been tending the fire dropped their torches and ran for the safety of the villages. They had no sooner turned their backs on the nighttime when another bonfire exploded next to them, those men also turning and running for the village. One fire after another burst into the cold night air as yells of warning pealed out through the village and its defenders. I saw the other men from all of the other bonfires rush in from their posts to reinforce their fellows at the makeshift barricades that surrounded the village. Their flight was hastened by the appearance of a lone figure, barely visible in the dimming coals of the bonfire. He stood alone, not even moving as the coals flickered around him.

"Prepare a volley!" I heard Saddhan's distinctive screech ring out in the night. As the men readied their weapons, their attention fully fixed on the lone figure that defied them, I noticed several dark shadows slip by the unattended bonfires behind them.

"If we all fire at once, he can't block them all." Saddhan announced, then drew another deep breath.

"Fire!" I heard the distinctive ring that came from all of the launchers being released at the same time. The shower of stones shot through the air, only visible as a passing grey puff of smoke in the night. The clanging of stones as they broke themselves against the figure was deafening for a mere second, then it was all over. The figure, thoroughly dented by the onslaught, tipped back and fell stiffly onto its back.

The yells coming from the village were not yells of outrage at having only demolished a metal decoy, however. The villagers yelped in surprise as the group of Destroyer shadows descended on them from the rear. The sounds of struggle were compounded by the roaring yells of the rest of the army as they rushed over the dying coals to assist in the battle.

The battle ended quickly. It was almost over by the time I had run in for a closer look. The men in the village already doubted their leader and their cause. The attack in the dark by those whom they had feared from their earliest childhood proved too much and they quickly folded to the oncoming army. Only Saddhan retained his launcher, which he had managed to reload, hiding while others fought. He now held several men at bay, pointing the weapon at each of them, threatening them in turn, his back to a corner. His eyes flashed with the insane rage that boiled inside as he realized his final defeat. He just couldn't decide whom he wanted to kill before he was taken.

Several men still thrashed. They were disarmed, but their hatred ran too deep to ever let them give up. Their arms were held by Destroyers as they struggled to free themselves, cursing everyone around them. Their hatred found a focus as Sadavir reached the barricade and stood on top of it, using it as a pedestal to address the crowd.

"We should have killed you when we had the chance, you

freak!" Even in the dim light, I could recognize the man who spoke, it was one of Padam's friends who had held my arms during Sadavir's last night in the village.

"Why?!" The tortured cry came from a man I didn't recognize, the pain of many years was evident in his eyes. "My son was killed by these animals! They never ceased their raids, even with the wall. Now you have sold us all out. Why?"

Sadavir's head hung for only a moment before raising again, the dancing light from the fires casting strange shadows on his face.

"The Destroyers were fighting for their survival because we left them to die. And if you are looking for someone to blame for the death of your son, maybe you should look to Saddhan."

"Saddhan, what is he talking about?" The man demanded. Saddhan looked up, his launcher still twitching around his many attackers. By now Sadavir had confirmed with André that it had been Saddhan who had been letting them through all those years ago. A few of the men of the army nodded, but not all of the Creators had been there when Sadavir had denounced Saddhan at the gate.

"He's lying! I haven't done anything!" Saddhan yelled, his voice breaking as he tried too hard to sound sincere and offended at the accusation.

"Saddhan was the one who let the Destroyers through. He used them as he used you. He let them through and then used your fear to control you."

"Saddhan, is this true?!" The man had completely forgotten about the Destroyers who held his arms and now twisted to face Saddhan, whose launcher now pointed at more and more people as Creators joined in surrounding the man. Saddhan didn't answer, knowing already that he would not be believed.

Olya climbed up over the barricade to see what was happening. Saddhan's eyes flicked over to the newcomer on the scene. Recognizing her, his eyes went to Sadavir, and a small smile started to form on his lips as he swung his launcher to point at Olya.

He had found his last victim.

His aim steadied and held for just a moment before he was slammed into the barricade wall by an invisible force that rippled in the night air. He was crushed into the stone wall and held there for an immortal moment before slumping to the ground. He didn't move again.

The crowd stared at the motionless body for several seconds before swinging their gaze to look at Sadavir. The two Stones were still clenched in his raised fist. He stood as motionless as the corpse on the ground. All struggling had stopped, not even crickets chirped in the still night air. The silence was broken by Andre's casual drawl.

"Well, that didn't turn out so bad."

The darkness of the night passed in silence, every man and woman was left to his or her own thoughts until they fell asleep wherever sleep took them. The sun rose on a new world. Skeptical eyes gazed in wonder as the army set to doing what they knew best. Houses were repaired, furniture that had been torn out of houses for the barricade were rebuilt in moments and strong arms lifted them back into their rightful spots. Whether the arms belonged to Creators or Destroyers didn't seem to matter much.

It wasn't a perfect world. Creators and Destroyers still glanced at each other nervously, still feared one another. But

231

when there was a task to be done, none found shame in accepting help from another. It was a beginning.

It didn't take me long to find Sadavir. Olya was at his side and he had a rare smile on his face.

"Do you see, Uncle? I think it's going to be all right."

"I suspect it will be. I have enjoyed this story." Something in my tone caught his attention and he turned from the friendly scene before him to face me.

"You're leaving, aren't you, Uncle?"

"Yes, my feet are starting to itch all over again, and I just have to see what is on the other side of those mountains."

"But don't you want to see how this story ends?" Sadavir pleaded.

"I already know how this story ends, Sadavir."

Sadavir smiled. "Can you see the future then, Uncle?"

"No." I responded. "But I can see the past, and that's just as good. I only want the answer to one more question, Sadavir."

"Name it, Uncle."

Grabbing his wrist, I led him away from Olya and any other listening ears.

"How did you feel when you killed Saddhan?" I whispered low.

"Uncle, please do not think me weak." Sadavir's tone was almost childlike. "But I felt sicker than I have ever felt before. The feeling hasn't left me yet, nor do I think it ever will. Am I a coward, Uncle?"

I smiled. "No, Sadavir, I do not think you weak. Don't worry, this story has a happy ending for as long as you lead this people."

A blank look flashed across Sadavir's face, followed by one

of terror.

"Lead? Uncle, what do you mean? I don't want to... I never... I'm just a..." He had obviously not considered his impact on the people past his short-lived military campaign. I again took his wrist and led him, stumbling, back to Olya.

"Don't worry, Sadavir, your queen will help you out immensely." Sadavir broke out of his worried mumblings to look confused.

"What do you mean, my..." Suddenly realizing what I meant, he smiled broadly, his black Stone making an odd contrast to the blush that spread over his face and down his neck. His blush still did not match Olya's, however, but she was also smiling.

"Well, I think my work here is done." I said.

"We will miss you, Uncle." Olya said as she quietly slipped her hand into Sadavir's. "Please come back to visit us sometime."

"I just might, Olya. I just might." I responded, knowing full well I would never see this land again. I turned my back on them and started my long walk towards the mountains. I heard heavy footsteps somewhere behind me and Aric's winded voice questioning his son.

"He's leaving?" And then raising his voice, he yelled after me.

"You're a conniving scoundrel and a lousy hand at the bellows, Amar! May your paths always be straight and lead you back to us soon."

I paused, turned, and waved goodbye. The last image I had was Aric pulling Lauria in close to his side as Olya helped Sadavir unclasp the armbands from his forearms. I would truly miss that family.

My feet soon carried me over the mountains and my eyes drank in the sight of new land. I was wandering again.

So that was the story of Sadavir, a man crafted for war and dedicated to peace. There are always lessons to be learned in every story. And I hope above all things that you realize this one simple truth:

This was a story about you.

About the Author

Lance Conrad lives in Utah, surrounded by loving and supportive family who are endlessly patient with his many eccentricities. His passion for writing comes from the belief that there are great lessons to be learned as we struggle with our favorite characters in fiction. He spends his time reading, writing, building lasers, and searching out new additions to his impressive collection of gourmet vinegars.

What happens when honor demands treason?

Two brothers, Simeon and Joseph, must join forces with Asher, a brutal man called Hunger by his enemies, to save their kingdom. Can they justify their actions when saving the kingdom means turning on the king himself?

Look for The Price of Nobility, coming out in print in 2014 from Dawn Star Press

For updates, follow author Lance Conrad on Twitter: @LanceConradlit